# A STORM
# WITHOUT RAIN

385

Varsity Reading Ser-

3195

# A STORM WITHOUT RAIN

.

## Jan Adkins

*A Beech Tree Paperback Book*

*New York*

Printed in the United States of America.

10  9  8  7  6  5  4  3  2  1

Library of Congress Cataloging-in-Publication Data

Adkins, Jan.
    A storm without rain / Jan Adkins. — 1st Beech Tree ed.
      p.    cm.
    Summary: While spending the day alone on an island near
his Cape Cod home, a fifteen-year-old suddenly finds himself
transported back in time where he is befriended by a boy
who will grow up to be his grandfather.
   ISBN 0-688-11852-6
   [1. Time travel—Fiction.   2. Cape Cod (Mass.)—Fiction.]
I. Title.
[PZ7.A2612St     1993]
[Fic]—dc20                             92-24601
                                             CIP
                                             AC

*I came to the Bay from Ohio, in company with a smart-mouthed Bay girl. I found most of what I love: strong friends, beautiful children, home. Most of my books came up that Bay with the wind, and the seasons, and some storms, too. One, worse than all the rest, took the Bay girl with it and changed the shape of the shore forever. When the storm was grayest and coldest there were friends who helped to clear away the wreckage and saw us through; this book is for them. It is a salute marred by bumbles and anachronisms. Perhaps when they read it these same flaws will remind them of me. I left the Bay going south, against the wind and all expectations, with another Bay girl and family in tow. But the Bay is still with me; I see it in my dreams and run the chart before I sleep: from Hen and Chickens and the doomed barge, across the mouth to Penikese and the independent republic of Cuttyhunk, all the way up two fascinating shores to Onset and the peevish currents of the Canal. I send the Bay my love, and Wareham, and Marion, and the Mothers:*

| | |
|---|---|
| Betsy | Joey |
| Maggie | Eileen |
| Betty | John |
| Bert and Sylvia | Peter |
| Marty and Colin | William and Virginia |
| Pat | Ann |
| Chris and Christine | Sandy and Charlie |
| Dick and Barbara | Jane and Bill |
| Matt | Jane |
| Pat | David and Joan |
| Judy and Michael | Skip and Daryl |
| Gordy and Linda | |

# CONTENTS

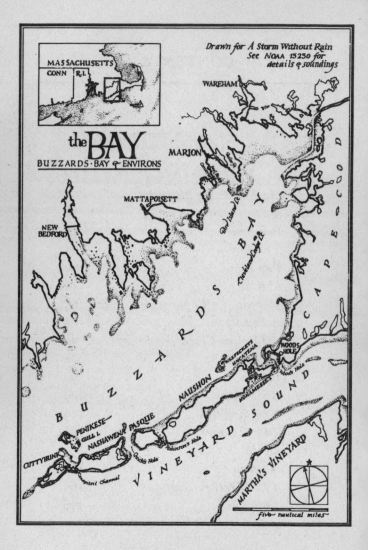

MASSACHUSETTS

CONN. R.I.

Drawn for *A Storm Without Rain*
See NOAA 13250 for
details & soundings

# the BAY
BUZZARDS · BAY & ENVIRONS

WAREHAM

MARION

MATTAPOISETT

NEW BEDFORD

Bird Island Lt.

B U Z Z A R D S   B A Y

Cleveland Ledge Lt.

WOODS HOLE

C A P E   C O D

NAUSHON

UNCATENA
NONAMESSET

PENIKESE
GULL I.
NASHAWENA   PASQUE

CUTTYHUNK

Robinson's Hole

Quick's Hole

Canapitsit Channel

V I N E Y A R D   S O U N D

MARTHA'S VINEYARD

five nautical miles

# A Storm
## without Rain

## CHAPTER ONE

# *Marion, Early Morning*

ALL THIS I'm about to tell you happened a long time ago, but sometimes I think it was only last August. There are times when it blurs, and if I don't tell you now, I'm afraid there will be a time when I won't believe any of it. When I remember that I once thought it was all true, I'll wonder about myself.

It happened, I'm sure of that today. The pictures in my mind are still fresh and crisp, still moving, and I remember the smells and sounds that go with them.

It happened in Marion. Marion is my town, my

family's town, and has been forever, give or take a generation. It seems curious that something like this could begin and go on and end in one place that isn't, wasn't, won't be the same place. You're right, I'm confused. But I'm sure it was Marion and I'm sure of the dates: it began on August the twentieth, my grandfather's birthday, and it ended . . . well, maybe I'm not so sure about that date. Maybe it hasn't ended.

It started with the party, John Swain Carter's ninety-third birthday, and I was ticked. My mother had organized an open house, and at the Big Moment in the afternoon, when all of John Swain's wheezing old friends were gathered around him for photographs, my sisters were to sing him a song and I — since I'm named after him — was to give a speech. Written by my mother. The whole thing gave me a pain. I was fifteen years old, I announced, and I was not going to read any sappy speech to a bunch of old people who wouldn't hear it anyway. My mother looked Stricken to the Heart and my father looked up from his newspaper and said I certainly would. My mother said it was a Great Honor to Grandfather Carter and wasn't I his namesake and it was Such a Little Thing to Do.

Doris is all right, as far as mothers go, but fairly gooey. My sisters said it would be a load of fun and what was the matter with me, anyway? They are both older sisters and they are not all right. Nothing whatever was wrong with me, I said; I did not enjoy singing cutesy songs in front of people or making sappy speeches and I wouldn't do either one. My mother put her hand over her heart (it's a move I think she learned from an old movie) and said to my father, William, Our Son! as if I had just passed away. Oh, it was too much.

Will buried himself in his newspaper, trying to make believe none of us were there, and that made me even angrier. I don't know why. If he'd stand up for me or lay down the law to me or just explain to me *why* I Certainly Would — but he just turned away from all of us. And Doris, damn, how dumb and sweet can you get without throwing up, telling everyone what to do as if none of us knew which way the bathroom was. Then my sisters. *Feh.* I got up and walked right out the kitchen door, ignoring my sisters, who were telling Doris what a brat I was in voices loud enough to kill mosquitoes. I did not know why anyone, least of all me, should be part of a family. Where did those people come from? I didn't understand any of them.

I was going to walk out onto the dock, but John Swain was out there under the little roofed-over bench, casting for bluefish.

It wasn't John Swain I was angry about. He wasn't a bad old bird. I liked him, really, though he

was another part of the family I just didn't understand. The way he'd spend half a day cobbling some
little thing out of wood, when he could walk over
and buy it new in the hardware store for fifty cents.
The way he insisted on living more or less alone in
the far part of this crazy house we all share. I guess
Carters have been living in the same house since
they came over to get things ready for the *May-
flower,* and every generation has tacked on some
shed or shop. The house is now in six or seven parts
and it all but surrounds Goosefish Cove. It was a
boat-building shop. You can just barely read the old
letters on the long shed:

CART R & SO , BOA WORKS.

I didn't really know because I had never been
interested in family trees or histories or any of that
stuff that sounded as sappy as the historical society
stuff Doris got into. Will sells boats but not the old
kind. Fiberglass runabouts and fishing skiffs, Sunfish,
boat trailers, and marine supplies out of a metal
building on Route Six.

Anyway, I didn't want to talk to John Swain,
being so mad about the party. I cut around behind
the yard and walked up Hiller Street to the drug-
store. It was late in the evening and they were just
closing down, turning off the lights and the sign.
Some of the kids from Tabor Academy were playing
Frisbee on Front Street under the streetlights. I

waved and went on. I just didn't want to talk, I guess. I walked past the cannon in front of the VFW hall, took a look at the geraniums in the old stone watering trough across the way (Doris had me hauling dirt for her when the Garden Club planted those things), and went up toward Spring Street. The pavement was black and smooth in the dark, then light gray in the streetlight spots that went smaller and smaller up to Sippican School. Bugs jigged around the lights. It felt good to walk and I was beginning to have a plan. I walked until late and went home.

Will and Doris were in their room with the TV on. My sisters were out, on dates I guess. I was quiet going up to my room, and I went to bed knowing what to do.

At about four in the morning on the day of the party I was up. I went through the kitchen and put some sandwiches in a bag, took a jar of juice and some bananas, and left before anyone was awake. It was the thin end of morning, the almost light before sunrise, dim enough that the lamp in John Swain's window was bright. He was up, too. As I walked out the dock I could see him moving around inside, making tea or something, I couldn't tell. Old people don't sleep well. I never went to bed after John Swain's light was out and never got up before him. I think he took naps in the afternoon.

I uncleated the lines and, not wanting to start the motor near the house, gave a push and let the Whaler drift out. It took a while; there wasn't a trace of breeze. The trees held their leaves against the sky without a move. Some ducks were being bothered in Hammett's Cove across the harbor, but otherwise there wasn't a sound. I looked back at the crazy angles of the boatworks, chowdered together over eight or ten generations. When I saw it again it would not look the same.

The Whaler drifted: the seventeen footer, nothing special, a runabout you can see anywhere there's water, but a boat that will scoot along when you push it. The motor is an old Johnson that starts every time because Will and I take care of it, one of the few things we do together. Will and I don't do a lot of talking. Sometimes we work on the motor or on a screen door or something for an hour without saying anything. It's not bad to be with him that way; it's as close as we get. The only rub is that it could be so much better. I'd like to know what he thinks about, whether I'm like he is inside or if he's completely different. I don't know what he and John Swain were like together either. Are Will and I supposed to play the same game they played? I had the sudden urge to go back and ask John Swain, making tea at five in the morning. He was a talker, John Swain; not a babbler like old guys who can't remember what they started to say, but interesting on some subjects. Not that we had much to talk about. John Swain was from another age. I didn't go back. But it's just as well.

I started that old Johnson and idled out the channel to Ram Island. It was getting light enough to see Marion, the lawns and houses, the yacht club and all the boats, hundreds, and the trees coming down to the water. Marion has a special color, I've always thought, a coolish browny green from the trees and the lawns. Once I was past the anchorage and Ram Island, I opened her up and was stepping when I passed the red nun. The Johnson was an old motor but big.

I cut along the shore, inside the markers but not too far. Even an outboard can run aground in there. At Converse Point I turned south, down toward the Islands. The Bay was smooth but not slick like in a dog-hot calm, just easy. The steady engine noise, the gentle rocking back and forth that came from the slow push and drop of the Whaler planing along, and the breeze from our own motion were pleasant, hypnotic. Sometimes you can get lost in the sound of a motor, it builds around you and you lose track of things. You think about things without trying. You may notice things happening — markers, islands going by — but they're far off and unrelated. You decide things without knowing it, you lose track of time and a long trip is suddenly at its end. And there I was, at Penikese Island, throttling down to make a landing.

It was just coming on to high tide. I made for the north beach, just where the cliffs end, cut the Johnson, and tilted it up. The Whaler glided into a sandy stop and I didn't have to get my feet wet.

My plan was to hang around Penikese most of the day. I'd leave the Whaler where she sat and in an hour she would be high and dry. When I went back in the evening I would tell Will and Doris just what happened: that I went fishing, beached the Whaler, and forgot about the tide. That I couldn't float her until six in the evening. Well, it would be very nearly what happened. I might even dig John Swain a mess of birthday clams. Clever, right?

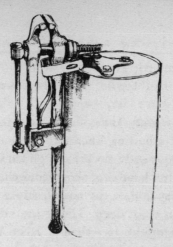

## CHAPTER TWO

# *A Storm without Rain*

**H**IGH AND DRY, the boat sat a good thirty feet from the water's edge, with a ledge of rocks between it and the water. I couldn't get it afloat if I'd wanted to, and I didn't. I was having a fine day.

At ten the wind had been up, southwest, as regular as clockwork, and would keep rising until two, then hold at eighteen to twenty knots until it stopped at five o'clock as if it were quitting time. These August days on the Bay are all alike, and the August days of one year are more or less interchangeable with another. The heat and humidity add a haze to the wind that cottons out the sight of the other shore. Bay people call a day like this a smoky sou'wester. Always have.

I untied a bailing bucket from the Whaler's seat and found a sandy pocket in the rocks that looked clammy. I took off my shorts and shirt (nobody is ever on that side of the island) and waded into the water about waist deep. The water is colder down at the mouth of the bay than it is in Marion at the head, but you can get used to it. I scrunched around with my toes in the sand until I felt the round, hard shells, dug them out with my feet, and reached down to pick them up. It's one of the best ways to clam. In half an hour I had a bucketful of cherrystones, the small, tender quahogs for eating raw. I rinsed them, poured the water out of the bucket (they'll drown in still water), and packed the top with wet rockweed to keep them cool. It was a good birthday present; John Swain would love them. What he didn't eat raw would go into a chowder. I put the bucket in the shade and went back to get some for myself.

Later I sat up the hillside against a rock, eating quahogs and washing them down with lemonade. I could save my sandwiches for evening. Drying in the sun after the cold water, hearing the sou'wester buffeting around my rock, I was feeling full from the clams, clean from the water, and sleepy from the sun and the early rising. Really sleepy. I pulled on my shorts and made a pillow of my shirt and leaned back against the rock to doze. For a while I watched two sailboats beating up from Woods Hole together, doing a long, slow dance in the wind and haze, and then I slept.

Sleep and half sleep: from time to time I would half wake and half notice the wind still up, half see a boat close inshore, hear part of a gull's cry. When you are caught between sleep and waking, thoughts sometimes come up out of the dark part of your head like random numbers. You hook them together in no special order, and they roll behind your eyes like a circus train with different cars full of animals and popcorn machines and freaks and generators and all painted crazy. And sometimes it's pleasant or even funny, sometimes warm and very interesting, sometimes disturbing. Half sleep, that's the way it was. Except that this time it got a little bumpier than it ever had been. And louder. Usually it's so quiet, but this got even bumpier and louder still; confused noise and jolting, but without the feeling of being jolted, if you can imagine that. It wasn't at all pleasant, to the point that I was trying to get out, get awake, but I was caught and it was like being caught underwater; no, more like being in the middle of a storm, a storm without rain — and then there were the sheep.

At first I saw just the one sheep standing in a
patch of grass, but only part of the time. It was like
fog blowing through; the sheep standing there chewing and then the picture shredding away, coming
back in parts, going away, coming back, but all the
time the sheep standing in the same place, chewing.
I didn't like it. There was a big gust of picture-fog,
or whatever, and a shudder, but without the jerk
of a shudder, if you know what I mean — it's hard
to tell about it — then the sheep standing there
plain and solid, still chewing and looking bored as
hell, and me feeling queer, and more sheep. The
noise was gone, though my ears still felt battered.
The other sheep, six or eight of them, huffed softly
and murmured to one another as they walked to the
clump of grass.

I sat, leaning against the rock, breathing hard and
my heart going. My eyes were wide open. I was glad
I was awake and afraid of being awake at the same
time. I raised my hand to wipe my forehead, and the
nearest sheep skittered back a few feet and bleated,
as if it hadn't noticed me till then.

I was beginning to calm down. Okay, I told myself, it's okay. Same day, same sou'wester, same
boats. More boats than when I went to sleep, but the
same bay.

I began wondering when the school on the other
side of Penikese had gotten sheep, when a couple of

things struck me about the boats. First, there were no fishing boats working the rocks, no motorboats at all. Second, the number of boats: they were all over the part of the Bay I could see in the haze, mostly small boats. Next, the sails were all gaff-rigged; they had four-sided sails in place of the triangular marconi-rigged sails I was used to seeing. Something odd in that. I could see a catboat up toward Pasque Island, and the two men in it were obviously pulling a lobster pot. Why, if the lobster boat that had set that pot motored around the island just then, there would be big trouble. I was amazed these guys dared to pull it in broad daylight.

Too many boats. It could have been an old-timer's race, but they were spread out here and there, beating and reaching and running in different directions. My stomach was cold and my heart was still going. It was all . . . not wrong, it looked too peaceful and purposeful to be wrong. *I* was wrong. Scared, too. It was especially bad because I had no real reason.

The sheep were bleating and all looking in one direction, up the hill behind me. I heard the footsteps coming. I froze against the rock. I don't think I breathed.

I heard the footsteps in the grass, unhurried walking; then in the rocks, uneven stepping from rock to rock; then from behind my rock, and the shepherd of Penikese Island leaned down and around to me.

We looked at each other and then I was running, stumbling, flailing up out of the rocks and through the grass, into and out of the water, running along the edge so fast, so terrified that my legs ran and I rode them, arms swimming the air. I still saw the shepherd's curious, sad eyes, but no nose, no ear, no fingers, only bandages, sores. I ran, I ran, I ran, and I do not remember where or when I stopped.

## CHAPTER THREE

# *Penikese*

I REMEMBER creeping back through the rocks in the afternoon. The sheep were gone and so was the shepherd. The tide was coming in. The Whaler was gone, without a mark in the sand where it had been. I felt the sand there: dry, undisturbed, with wisps of half-buried seaweed. No boat had touched it that day, yet . . .

My bucket of clams and my jar of lemonade were still beside the rock. My hand shook as I picked the jar up. The lemonade was warm and sweet. The cap said A & P. The rockweed over the quahogs was still moist.

The boats on the bay moved slowly. It must have been about three o'clock. There was Nashawena, all right, and Pasque beyond it, light gray in the haze. I knew where I was, but I didn't. Something was wrong.

Bells. Shaking, I moved up the hill carefully, toward the sound. There were sheep droppings all through the bushes. I crawled on my hands and knees near the brow of the hill, then crept lower on elbows and belly into the tall grass at the crest. I began to raise myself to look, but I was shaking too much. I lay in the grass trying to breathe normally until the shaking passed. Then I looked.

The buildings I remembered were gone. There were a dozen other buildings in their place: shingled, peaked, chimneyed cottages and buildings of two and three stories, sheds, a dock at which lay a steamboat — yes, a steamboat — of about thirty-five feet with smoke blowing away from her stack. It looked liked a dolls' village, except the dolls, about twenty of them, were bandaged, limping, working their way unsteadily toward the dock. Barrels and boxes were being unloaded, there, and a bell was tolling. Some of the dolls crowded around the dock. Some went into the building of the bells. Was it a chapel?

Beyond, across the strait, lay Cuttyhunk, but not the island I knew. Most of the docks were gone, the old coast guard station out on the point was fixed up, and a flag was flying in the breeze that spun a dozen windmills. The Pond was strewn with small sailboats nosing up into the wind, and outside the Pond were four unbelievable boats: three schooners with green hulls and yellow markings and black bands along their deck lines, and, anchored apart from the schooners, one long, white, portholed, flag-fluttering steam yacht. I'd seen pictures of them in dusty frames at the boatworks: sword bows, signal masts, smokestacks. That anyone could restore one, much less steam around in it, was incredible.

The dolls finished with the unloading on the Penikese dock. My mind still wasn't working right. The bandaged doll-people, the sails, the yacht, the schooners, the shepherd . . . it was too much to understand.

The boat let its lines go and the little steamboat blew her whistle three times before she began to back slowly off. All the sailors who had been unloading cargo had, I could see now, been wearing gloves. Before the boat was clear they all took their gloves off and threw them back on the dock, then hurried forward into the pilothouse as the steamboat swung and started away. The doll people who clustered around the dock limped forward and picked up the gloves and matched them into pairs. Many of them wore gloves already, some required only one glove, some did not require gloves. I knew now. They were lepers.

The shepherd's leprous face, his bandages. The chapel, the cast-off gloves. Something John Swain had said about Penikese: "It was a leper colony, at one time, you know. I remember when they closed it down in '24." 1924. The schooners, the steam yachts, the sails.

I dropped into the grass and spun around. The boats were still on the bay. I felt sick. I realized there would be no motorboat to stop the catboat from pulling lobster pots. The pots belonged to the catboat. A deep whistle sounded and I watched, terrified, as a great, gaudy steamboat passed, funnels throwing smoke back along the wind, lettered NEW YORK PACKET. The New York Packet hadn't run in forty-five years.

The troubled sleep, the storm without rain, they had brought me here. Where? The same place I began. I had been carried by a storm in a dimension not of height and width and depth, but of time. A time storm had brought me . . . not where, but *when*.

Another sail, very close ashore, was rounding the point. I was trapped on a leper colony in a year sometime before I was born. I forgot everything real

I'd ever learned about leprosy and remembered only the fear of it. It is one of the least contagious diseases, but now I ran from it, down the slope and onto the beach, ran to meet the sail, to get off the island, to get anywhere but Penikese.

The boat under the sail was one of the ghastliest sights I'd ever seen, a small craft shaped like a pumpkin seed, from what I could see. The low, rounded decks were heaped with dead things: ducks and geese, mostly, but also some muskrats and snapping turtles and a fox. Wherever you could see a patch of deck it was stained, with blood. The man in it steered with one hand, for he had only one arm. He didn't seem to be a leper, though: no bandages, no sores, the clothes rough, and the shoulder of his shirt sewn right across with no provision for a sleeve. He seemed a powerful man, anything but sickly, tanned leather dark with tufts of his brown hair bleached from the sun. He was a grim man: his unshaven face was as dead as his cargo. I rushed toward his boat, scrambling out a point of rocks. He did nothing. "Get me out of here!" I called, floundering in the water, trying to reach him. "Get me away from this place!"

His face did not change, he did not move his tiller an inch until I was a boatlength away, chest deep in the water. Then he let go the tiller and swung out a double-barreled shotgun from beside his leg. I was looking directly down both black bores and I heard two distinct clicks as he cocked the hammers.

"Git," he said, his voice without a trace of concern. "Git back where you b'long. Away from clean folks. You lepers want all of us sick and rotting. Git!"

The grisly boat glided past. He raised his shotgun and held it muzzle up, the barrels leaning against his shoulder. I stood in the water watching him go until I began to shiver.

Later I shivered in the grass, though it was warm. I was frightened and lost. Lost is the worst feeling I can imagine. When I was little I got separated from Doris in a very large supermarket. I wandered through long aisles banked with armies of soup cans, walls of soap boxes, past forests of celery and broccoli, familiar stuff but overwhelming in numbers, the rank-on-rank sameness, the uneatable supply of cereal. In the frozen-food section it was cold; I began to shiver and cry. Shoppers crowded around me, trying to help, but blocking out the world and any hope of finding Doris with a circle of strange bodies. I had nowhere to go and remember even now the awful thought of living in the supermarket forever, not knowing any of the people who clattered past with their carts. I would eat uncooked food from the boxes (I could not open cans, then). I was so terrified that I didn't even resist the strange arms as they picked me up and carried me, limp and crying, to the manager's stall. Doris found me there. I remember how angry and relieved I was, though all I could do was cry. She shouldn't lose me! I was only a small boy who couldn't even open cans. It is the worst feeling, being lost, and I had it shivering on Penikese, wishing Doris would come and pick me up. I was fifteen years old but I didn't feel it. I wanted to go home.

But I had no home. Or did I? Doris and Will were gone . . . or weren't yet . . . that was too complicated to worry over, though. I was alone in a world I knew nothing about, and the only place I had any ties of warmth and familiarity was Goosefish Cove and the Carter boatworks. I knew that when I saw the crazy angles of that hodgepodge I would feel better. That's where I would go.

There's no better cure for fright than a plan. A good plan, a bad plan, an incomplete plan, any plan. I had something to work at, and that would hold me for a while. When I began to act on my plan I saw how much work there was to do.

## CHAPTER FOUR

# The Bay

I CRAWLED up to the crest again and I worked on my first problem. The only way back to Marion was on a boat from Cuttyhunk. What would take me to Cuttyhunk? Between Penikese and Cuttyhunk lay a mile of cold water that would be ebbing out to sea at night, and the current would be considerable. I couldn't swim it.

There's more than one way to skin a cat. That's what John Swain always said, and there was another way to swim the channel. Instead of going directly south to Cuttyhunk, I could swim east to Gull Island, just a little pile of rocks a few hundred yards off Penikese. I could see the waves working around it now and knew it would be calm by night. These August days were all alike. From Gull I could wade a long way, then, toward Nashawena Island. A half-mile swim, probably, but then I could walk down the beach to Canapitsit Channel and swim that easily, only a hundred yards or so. Penikese to Gull to Nashawena to Cuttyhunk: I looked it over carefully, remembering that it would look different at night, then lay back in the grass and tried to sleep. I didn't do very well.

By nightfall I was ready. I had my jar of lemonade strapped to a driftwood plank with my belt, and my sneakers tied beside. I would paddle the plank ahead like the flutterboards they used in swimming lessons. It turned out to be a very good thing. It was a long night.

I don't like swimming at night in the ocean. There's something evil about black water under you. But that night I didn't mind it; I suppose I was too scared about my whole situation to be afraid of dark water. If I did today what I did that night, so very long ago, I would be a basket case. If I felt weeds and floating things touching my legs, as they did that night, I would yell until all Cuttyhunk could hear me. That night I kept swimming under half a moon. At Gull Island I waded in my sneakers, slipping on the rocks, and being careful not to cut myself because blood in the water might attract sharks, but I was not afraid. Amazing.

The swim from Gull to Nashawena was even longer than I thought it might be. I don't think I could have made it without the plank. I swam and rested on it, swam and rested. I drank some of the lemonade, which helped, but all I could do was keep paddling on. I may have paddled farther than I had to, because when I touched bottom unexpectedly and stood up, it was only three feet deep.

As I walked slowly along the beach I noticed that I was tired, but not overwhelmed with panic or sadness. Nothing is ever as bad as it seems from the outside. There was even a tingle of adventure to it, walking alone on the beach at night, swimming channels and hiding. It was like a spy movie, but there was no popcorn, and I knew no comfortable words would flash on a screen when it was over: "The end."

The current in Canapitsit Channel wasn't a big problem; I must have caught it at near slack. Even so, it swept me along the Channel toward the Bay a hundred yards and it was cold. I reached shore and finally lay down. In the morning I woke up under a bush, curled into a cramped, cold, damp bundle. It was not a pleasant waking, partly because I wanted it all to be a dream and to find myself back in my own bed when I woke.

I walked along the sand, stretching out my kinks, hungry and still cold. Small boats were sculling and rowing out the channel in the morning calm. I was hungry.

"Well, Jack," I said to myself, and the sound of my own voice startled me, "you've got to earn breakfast and a boat ride." I had four dollars and seventy-five cents in money I couldn't use until about 1950, and a pocketknife with one blade dulled from opening quahogs. I was wearing a tennis shirt, cut-offs, and wet sneakers. I headed for the docks.

Her name was lettered across her broad catboat transom: ALLISE, and her call under it, MARION. Sweet smells and smoke drifted out of her stubby stovepipe.

"Hello?" I called.

"Yes sir?" a voice replied from the cabin.

"Excuse me, but could I have a word with you?"

He rose out of the companionway putting on his hat, a derby, and before he stepped up on deck or said another word, he slipped his coat on, so that when he stood before me he was dressed with a dusty black formality. "Whom do I have the honor of addressin'?" he asked. It was my first exchange of words with anyone from this new — or old — world. Conversation across a shotgun doesn't count.

"Jack Stone," I said, and seeing him standing stiffly in his coat and vest and derby, I added, "sir." I do not know why I suddenly chose *Stone.*

"And I am Corbin Starkweather, pleased to make your acquaintance. What can I do for you, Jack my boy?"

He was a small man with a hearty voice that seemed to come from a great walrus mustache that twitched and puffed as he spoke. His hands were large and stained but he had small feet, and though his suit was frayed at the cuffs and collar, he looked, well, *dapper,* a word I could not have applied to anyone from my own time.

"I was hoping to earn passage to Marion," I said; then, looking at the smokestack, added, "and hoping I might earn breakfast, too, sir."

He was looking at my clothes and I felt very out of place.

"Where do you hail from, Jack Stone?"

"I'm an orphan, sir." This was as far as I'd worked my story out.

"That don't answer my question, Jack."

"New York, sir. I was working on a boat sailing up from New York and decided to get off here."

His eyes, sharp brown eyes, narrowed. "Did you jump ship?"

"Yes, sir." I seized at anything, now. "The cook was mean to me. I'm trying to get to Marion because we put in there, once, and it seemed like a fine town."

He hesitated. "Is that all you are running from?"

"Yes, sir."

"Are you given to tobaccos, spirits, or degrading habits?"

I thought for an instant he was joking, but saw at once that he was serious.

"I try to take care of myself, Mr. Starkweather. I don't drink or smoke."

He looked at me hard, then gave a quick nod, just a jerk of his head. "Very well, Jack Stone. I ain't in the business of employing helpers, but I am taking a load of clams to the Marion Hotel. If you will work the barrels with me on both ends you shall have passage and meals. You may come aboard, Jack."

"Thank you, Mr. Starkweather."

I dropped down to his deck and followed him into his low cabin, where he took off his coat, stooping, but left his hat on. Without a word he sat down beside a small coal stove and wrapped a towel around his middle, and in fifteen minutes we had a breakfast such as I'd never eaten before: flakes of cod fried with eggs and thick slices of bread in pork fat and onions, hot, dark tea, and sweet condensed milk. We rinsed our plates in a bucket of salt water, wiped them with a sheet of newspaper, and Stark-weather said, "Now to work."

We worked, all right, manhandling eight barrels of softshell clams into place on the broad deck of the cockpit. By the time they were stowed and tied in place, the breeze was up some and we left Cutty-hunk Pond. Only when we had cleared the harbor did he take off his coat, but his derby and vest remained in place all through the day. The night swim and the work had me sore and tired, but I could not sleep on deck as Mr. Starkweather suggested because the Bay, my own bay, was such a spectacle. I had never imagined how it could be. It was alive!

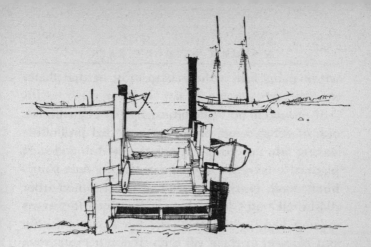

# CHAPTER FIVE

## Bay Life

THE BIRDS. Hundreds of them, thousands. That was the first thing I noticed. Gulls, of course, wheeling in the high-up vulture circles that gave Buzzards Bay its name, and flocks of them working the water, dipping and rising. Ducks, too. Great rafts of ducks floated in the shallows, covering acres, more than anyone could count. There were two directions of terns, one skimming low, sinking between the wave tips, flying away from shore, and the other flying steady and straight toward the rocks, carrying tiny fish in their sharp bills; fighter planes out, transports home. I saw a dozen osprey with their proud tan-on-white plumage and their still, flat span of wing; some soared, some carried profitable-looking fish, nose forward, tail aft, the fish and bird together looking like a good design for a float plane. There were Mother Carrie's chickens, those little quail-sized water birds that live between the waves and can hardly fly, just flitter over crests. I'd only seen pictures of them till then. It was a prosperous community of birds and it had a king.

It was so close, so big, that I could see it flex the broad wings and tip its trailing feathers in the gusts. It came from behind us, riding fast on the wind, and its shadow crossed me, as big as a rug. The sun behind it for that instant set it on fire, golden. I turned to Corbin Starkweather. "Is that a golden eagle?"

"Yessir. It's a golden. Big, ain't he?" He held a fist into the sun to look toward it. "His end of the Bay. Up to the Onset end, that's a bald eagle. You have never seen it?"

"No, sir."

"Grand sight. Big fellow. Emblem of the Union, a real scrapper. Not so common now as when I was a boy." When he was a boy. I looked into the water going past. I'd wiped my plate with a newspaper printed on August 4, 1904. When he was a boy the

Civil War had just been fought. Emblem of the Union.

The water ahead of us broke in a long, hissing ruffle. Fish. I sat up. Gulls swung down toward us. The water broke closer to us and the silver sides of the baitfish flashed as they leaped, first one way and then another. We were on them now, parting them with our bow. They were deep and close, they were layered and ranked going down darker and greener, then something ripped through the pattern and they broke the surface right under me. I looked aft and, in the glare, there was a slick of oil, and gulls fetching bits.

"It is just as well to make this passage pay," Corbin Starkweather announced. "Take the wheel, if you will."

He reached under a seat and laid out hand lines in the cockpit, brown cord done up in large, even loops that relaxed and spread flat when he untied them. Corbin Starkweather, from the moment I first saw him, did everything in a quiet, neat, and entirely practical way that was almost dazzling. I steered, while he fetched a preserves jar out of the cabin filled with water or brine and dead-white strips — pork rind, I think. In less than a minute he was at the wheel again and we were both letting coils of line slip back over the side after baiting double hooks with a tail of split rind.

The hits came almost at once, almost together. Mine was a tremor, a tug, and then a terrific pull that surprised me into stumbling. I'd fished all over the Bay, but I'd never been attached to anything like this. The line was straight and tingling, it swept across to the right, a tug, then left.

"Bring him! Bring him!" Corbin shouted, and he was taking his line in, hand over hand in regular lengths that fell behind him in new coils. Apparently this wasn't a time to play fish out; this was a time to get fish in, this was business. The sail was luffing above us, loud, and the boat, which had nosed up toward the wind as soon as he had let go the sheet and the wheel, hardly moved. I was still working along the line, heaving it in as it swept back and forth, when I heard a smacking and pounding in the cockpit with us. Corbin must have boated his fish. A heavy, wet crack, then another, then no more pounding and I was still bringing it in. I stopped. Big, it was big as a submarine, and lunging around, angry. It was right there.

"Pull! Bring it home!" Corbin reached across me and took the line. "Pull!" he shouted and we both pulled. A long, angry, monster bluefish came out of the water and Corbin's gaff came down and hit it like a club; blood drops hung in the air, and we were all — Corbin and bluefish and I — stepping back, and the awful thing was sliding across the seat, arching and rearing its blue-green enormous length and hitting the cockpit decking while the gaff clattered in the corner. But Corbin had a real club, fat and heavy, and as the bluefish whipped its side at the boards, the club was poised high waiting for a clear shot, then came down, clapped behind the fishy eye, hard, then again, and the fourth time there was only stiff quivering. There was blood on my shins, from the gills. Corbin was kneeling with the club up, ready, like an axe murderer. I let out my breath. "Good lord."

". . . be praised. No swearin', Jack. Get that line out again." This was business.

So we fished. We got the hooks out of their toothy mouths with a notched dowel and spun the wheel and hauled in the sail with the boat running up the Bay again. We let out the lines (mine always got tangled, Corbin's ran out smooth each time) and brought in bluefish as long as the gulls were with us and the baitfish worried the surface. Then the fish were gone. We had fifteen big blues, two and three feet long, but my first blue was bigger, almost four feet and weighing easily thirty pounds.

Corbin slipped a loop of the main sheet over a wheel spoke. "Good work, a good half hour's work, Jack. We will see a profit from this. The hotel will serve bluefish this evenin'."

He set up a board that hung out over the starboard side, and put away the pork rinds. He made up his hand line in the same neat coils, then untangled mine and made it up. "You'll learn to drop them right as you bring in," he said, working with the line and balancing to the Bay chop with his knees and hips. "Oh, there's a science to everythin'." He looked to the sky. "Six or seven o'clock."

"Huh?" He looked sharply at me and I said, "I beg your pardon, sir?"

"Your manners are a touch rusty, Jack, and you would do well to polish them up for folks ashore. But you are a good-hearted boy, that is clear, and not afraid of work."

"Thank you, sir."

"The rain, six or seven o'clock. That's when it will start. Not much, but enough to rinse these lines if I hang them out." He tied a canvas apron over his vest and trousers.

"Yes, Mr. Starkweather." If I were back with Will and Doris (who would be skeptical at the idea that I wasn't afraid of work), I would call him Corbin. We had been together for hours. But the formal way he addressed me and the way he spoke to me — not unfriendly, not even formal — made me want to call him Mr. Starkweather. It fitted, and it was a form of respect for both of us. As for the work, there it was again, that respect business; it was plain that he expected me to work and do as good a job as

I could. I realized with surprise it was his idea of me as a worker that made me work. And the work never stopped.

First I hoisted fish up to the cutting board, then I hoisted water. As he gutted the fish with one knife and scaled them with another, I flipped a wooden bucket into the water and swung it aboard (it takes a knack to get it up without getting pulled over the side). When he was finished with a fish, I sluiced off the board, washing guts and scales overboard. We had cleaned about ten fish when I saw the sharks.

"Sharks!" I yelled.

Mr. Starkweather jumped. He recovered and said testily, "Jack. Don't go yellin' without a good reason or you'll be scarin' folks."

I pointed back in our wake and croaked out, more quietly, "Sharks."

"Well, yes, but we can't do a thing with them today because I don't have no shark hooks and no chain leader, and, beside, they are a *tussle* to boat. Yessir." He went on cleaning bluefish while the sharks went on snapping up the leavings. Blue sharks, they were, and all of ten feet. Corbin Starkweather gave them a glance from time to time, looking at lost profit I guess, and murmured something about laying some shark gear aboard.

All morning we ran up along the Elizabeth Islands, past Quick's and Robinson's and Wood's

Hole, and up toward Marion. Sails paraded the
horizon, sails of all shapes: two squarish spritsails
over a slim workboat working across the wind
would swing below another catboat like ours, with
its one gaff-rigged sail hard on the wind. Several big,
powerful-looking schooners rushed down to us and
tacked near the shore, staysails and jibs and flying
jibs and what-all fluttering, while the thick booms
creaked across and the transoms tipped and left the
surface swirling as they and their crew moved away
under a lawn-sized spread of patched canvas. In the
distance, once, I saw a great array of gaffs and yards
and jibs on (I thought) a topsail schooner. There
were a few steamers, but mostly small boats with
one or two men, workboats, dipping and sliding
across the Bay. We saw porpoise and small blackfish
whales, ocean sunfish, jellyfish. We saw cormorants
on the rocks and deer in the marshes. It was my
Bay, and it was beautiful.

We were running the western shore, then, and
passing West Island close in. The marshes were full
of ducks: a thousand on this side of a point and
another thousand or two thousand beyond it. They
didn't seem to mind us as we came by, and you
could hear them babbling away. We'd covered the
bluefish with a wet cloth and put away the cutting
board, and I was finally, with the murmur of the

water and the ducks and the shifting of the little inshore waves, about to sleep.

When, *wham, bam,* and the ducks all kicked off the water at once. Then again, *wham, bam,* and just after the second shot, something hit our sail like a handful of gravel. The ducks were all over the sky, the noise was terrific, but over it Corbin Starkweather was bawling in a voice astonishingly loud, "Dammit, Higgins!" He looked at me crouching down behind the rail and lowered his voice long enough to say, " 'Scuse me, Jack, forgot myself." Then bellowing again, "Higgins, you watch where you're pointin' that dad-blamed twelve-bore, twice-barreled bird killer. It ain't no —" He sputtered and clenched one fist and the situation got the better of him. "It ain't no *damned* wonder you have blown yourself to tatters. I am giving you fair warning, Higgins!"

A patched and soiled sail swung up over the marsh grass. There was something familiar and nasty in the way it raised up in separate jerks. We moved along the marsh and it moved in the marsh. Corbin Starkweather was muttering and looking at his sail where birdshot had hit it. The marsh sail fluttered and paused, tightened and came on. Skirting the rocks and grass of the marsh, we were coming closer to the sail and the boat hidden in the reeds. I didn't like it. Something remembered and wrong rattled in my head. Corbin Starkweather muttered, the wind shifted, we opened onto a reach of marsh inlet where the new wind brought out the low-tide smell of rotting mud and crab holes, and there it was: the dead boat, the same grisly boat I had seen on Penikese, piled even higher with ducks and geese, the same one-armed figure sitting low among them, shotgun butts showing near his waist. "Who is that?" I whispered.

"That," said Corbin Starkweather, speaking as if he were handling a spider, "That is One-armed Higgins. He is a market gunner, a drunkard, a scofflaw, a godless disgrace, and hardly human. He has run foul of me and of the town too many times. He deserves a public whipping or jailing or worse."

The dead boat swept past a mallard splayed out on the water. I watched Higgins lean and scoop it up and toss it onto the pile. He steered on with a stick that went aft to the rudder head. When he let it go, the boat and its pile began to veer. He brought a bottle up and took a pull, shoved it down beside him, and steered on to the next dead duck. He knew we were there but he didn't bother to look up. He didn't care that we were there.

"Higgins," called Starkweather. "Higgins! You have flouted your reckless ways long enough! You will have cause to rue this day!"

I crouched in the cockpit, hoping he wouldn't look up, hating him for not looking up.

"Higgins!"

But he was gone, farther into the marsh, only his dirty sail showing behind the reeds. As we sailed on toward Marion, that, too, slackened, paused, fell, and was gone. One-armed Higgins sat behind us somewhere in the marsh, waiting with his shotguns and his bottle amid his pile of feathers and flesh for more kills. He was a man who had called me a leper, a man who might do something about it.

Clouds overtook us from the southwest and the day was no longer bright.

We rounded Converse Point an hour later and it was all wrong. Maybe you'll grow old and after a long time come back to where you lived, and it will all be changed. I hope you never will. It was not just like that for me but near as bad.

The trees where gone. I could recognize the patterns of land but not the colors without them. I saw fields everywhere, separated by stone fences, with clumps and gatherings of trees here and there, often around houses. It looked desolate. The fields were growing, the fences were neat and kept up, from what I could see offshore, but the scene was bare and harsh. I saw a few cows, more than a few horses. The land breeze came out to us as we turned inside the point. It carried the smell of manure, not unpleasant but unexpected. A man on a handsome black horse waved to us from the road that approached the point beach from inland. I saw windmills turning and weathervanes on the white houses. It was all different.

I would have thought my town would look more countrified at the turn of the century, greener. It was browner, barer, and all the stone fences were like bones on the land. As the man on the horse rode inland, white puffs of dust came up from the hooves and drifted back onto the road.

Corbin Starkweather and I had not spoken since Higgins disappeared into the marsh. I was trying to coax myself out of feeling so low. Of course it's all different, I told myself, but it didn't do much good. I thought of the Bay, how alive it was, and that helped. Then a rock toward the shore moved and changed shape. It was a seal!

The charts had always given this rocky stretch of the outer harbor as "Seal Rocks," and now I knew why. There was a seal.

"Look," I said, "a seal."

It was as cute and as fat as any of the Boston aquarium seals. It had a dark tan coat brindled with black spots, and a light tan belly. We were close enough to see its pudgy, whiskered face and its big eyes. It looked playful and sweet.

The wheel was lashed. Corbin Starkweather ducked into the cabin. He came back up with a long sheepskin case, unbuttoning one end. He was watching the seal as he drew out the rifle and, dropping the case, brought it up to his shoulder.

"What are you doing?" I demanded.

He leaned lightly against the cabin, took the slight motion of the boat in his hips, brought back the hammer, and, just as expertly as he did everything else, squeezed off a single shot. The seal's head dropped onto the rock and its body shivered. The crack and ring of the rifle were in my ears; the wind was carrying away the muzzle smoke.

"What? Why did you do that?" I shouted. "Why the hell did you do that? Why shoot the seal?" He stooped and slid the rifle back into its case. He stepped to the wheel and threw off the lashing.

"Ready about," he said with a frown. "Get ready to help me get it aboard."

I stepped back to him and shouted in his face, "You get your own goddamned seal aboard, you goddamned —"

Suddenly I was crumpled up in the corner of the cockpit feeling the same way I had when I touched the sparkplug on the lawnmower, except now my face hurt and stung. Corbin was leaping nimbly about the cockpit and the sail was luffing, then he was gone forward and the sail came down over me and my side of the cockpit.

The boat stopped gently. I could hear Corbin Starkweather splashing in the water. I reached up to feel my face, which was beginning to throb. The boat tipped, Corbin wheezed, and with a great thump, the dead seal came rolling over barrels of clams and into the cockpit at my feet. A few minutes later we were under way again.

Mr. Starkweather didn't say a word, but his face was set.

I had gone too far. If you are ever in a place where you need every friend you can get, you might have to swallow some big, bitter bites. I did.

"Mr. Starkweather," I said. He didn't reply or even look at me as he sailed on. "Mr. Starkweather, I was way out of line back there and I apologize. I think things are a little crazy for me now but, even so, I shouldn't have insulted you."

He looked at me fiercely for a moment, then he said, "Jack, I don't know where you have hailed from or who has raised you or what troubles you have been in and I ain't asked. Wherever you are from you ought to be better raised than to profane your elders or to question how a man provides for his family." He took one hand off the wheel and pointed down at the seal. "But you ain't no bad boy. Whatever troubles you have, I do not believe there has been wickedness. You have been straight and manly with me just now by shouldering up to your mistake and I ain't going to neglect my Christian duty. I am givin' you the benefit and sayin' that you are forgiven."

He held out his hand that had been pointing down and we shook hands over the dead seal. "Thank you, Mr. Starkweather. I'm grateful." And I was.

We were coming into Marion now, past Ram Island. Except it was Marion as I'd never known it, and I would need every friend I could keep.

## CHAPTER SIX

# *Marion*

TELLING YOU THIS makes me feel old.
I say to you, "I remember Marion as it was
when . . . ," and I feel like some old codger wheezing
away about the old days. Maybe I know how they
feel now, having the past locked in them, or maybe it
really is different for me. But I remember. The land-
scape was bare but the village itself had more trees
than I thought it could have; it was a high green
garden.

I helped Corbin Starkweather unload his barrels,
rolling them up onto the grass-tufted town wharf

with a doubled line — parbuckling, he called it. The way he did it made the work easy and I was grateful for the excuse not to go directly into the town. But it was done too soon.

"We have had an eventful, productive passage, Jack, and that's for certain." He was hanging up his apron in the cabin and putting on his coat. His derby was still firmly on his head. "I am wishin' you well, here, and saying that you may ship with me on the occasions I need help. You are down on your luck," — he looked at my shorts and sneakers and T-shirt — "which is where, but for the Grace, we would all be.

"Anticipatin' a modest profit from this day's work and considerin' your predicaments, the advance of a dollar seems proper. That and Mrs. Starkweather's fare — if you need it, no offense meant — will keep you out of the tramphouse." He brought a silver dollar out of his coat pocket. I took it and thanked him. "Spring Street, near the Preacher's Rock, is where you can find the Starkweathers, Jack." He held out his hand, I shook it, and he said, "Cast me off, if you will."

The *Allise* drifted off the dock with the wind, and as Corbin Starkweather brought up the tip of the gaff and a corner of the sail, she seemed to rush away too quickly. He only needed a corner of sail to reach across the channel, and he dropped it far short

of his mooring, coming up on his dinghy not with a
sporty swoop but an easy, practical drift. When I
turned and walked off the wharf, he was still swab-
bing down *Allise* in his vest and derby.

As I walked into the shadow of the low buildings
on the land, I knew that I had avoided looking at
Goosefish Cove and the Carter Boatworks, directly
behind me all the time I was unloading barrels. I
never glanced at them. As I passed walkways between the sheds and buildings, I couldn't force myself to look through them and see the place. I
couldn't. In a hundred yards I stood on Front Street,
trembling. This was going to be hard. The Civil War
monument stood before me, but the cannon
memorializing World War I artillery dead that I
remembered wasn't there. There was a snort and a
splashing, as a horse drank noisily from the stone
trough, which was not filled with the Garden Club
geraniums for which I'd carried dirt. The horse continued to drink, its tail switched away flies, and the
carriage behind it sat without moving while its
driver waited. The driver tipped his derby hat. "How
de do," he said.

"Yes," I replied. I wanted to run.

I must have looked like a fool to him. Damn. I
stood there gaping as if it were a gold horse drinking
champagne. The driver was far more polite. He sat

and accepted the stare of what he must have thought of as a half-dressed half-wit without frowning or turning away. He spoke to his horse in a calm, patient voice: "Drink neat, Filo. Fellah here is admiring your style."

I should have gotten over it, talking to Corbin Starkweather, but no. It suddenly hit me that the man who spoke had undoubtedly been long dead and laid down in the Marion cemetery when I left Goosefish Cove in the Whaler. Was I hearing a ghost? His voice was too real, too local, with the broad *a*'s and clipped syllables of Yankee dialect. His black suit and worn watch chain, the flies embroidering the air around Filo's bony head, the quiet sounds of leather harness as the horse raised his head and backed a step away from the stone trough, it was all too real. Was I the ghost, staring at reality without a part in it?

"G'day to ya," he said with a smile. He clucked to Filo and, hitched together, they moved off down the street, Filo dropping a great horse ball behind him in the street.

I would still be there staring at that horse ball, unable to move, watching greenbottle flies collect around it, if it weren't for the bicycle, one of the high-wheel/low-wheel kind that I was to learn was called an ordinary. Maybe it was the tall shakiness of the thing, or the silly cap its rider was wearing; maybe it was the way the dirt road jarred the rider, a guy of about twenty with a long nose and a wide mustache, or maybe it was the way the cycle ran dead center through Filo's horse ball and threw little bits up on the rider's pants. Whatever. The bicycle's passing broke me out of my mood, and I said to nobody in particular, "Oh, hell, this is one weird mess, Jack." And I followed the bicycle and Filo and bits of horse droppings up the road.

As I walked, I thought about the Bay, the water and the islands and the wind. And I thought about horse balls and bicycles and silly caps, and turned down Hiller Street. I thought about being a part of the Bay and the town, and about the things that change and the things that don't change. At the end of Hiller I stood in front of my own home.

We'd let it go like a shrub, our old house, let it grow any way it wanted, into garages and clothes-line yards and garbage-can lattices and sheds for the lawn furniture. Now I saw it leaner. It still had purpose running through it. It looked like a working place, a provider, half shop and half home. I saw that the changes we had — *would* make were not building the place but covering it up, painting it over, closing it down. Why had my father let it go? There was the sign, dark green, with handsome cream letters:

CARTER & SON · BOATWORKS.

I was sitting there under a tree looking at the boat-works and there were tears in my eyes and I wanted to get back. I had no idea how I'd do it but I wanted to try. It was the boatworks as much as anything; that place was mine. I sat and tried to fix all the details of the place in my head. It started to rain.

My tree leaked. At first it was just a sprinkle, but then it came on to a real, earnest pour. I stood up and against the trunk, watching the water spout out of the wooden gutters and into the street. I didn't mind it, really. It had been building up to rain all day, and now that it was here, it was a kind of relief; but the fellow in the doorway minded for me.

He came out onto the breezeway through one of the shop doors and stood there looking at me, his hands in his shop apron, his features broken and blurred by water sheeting off the roof. I looked back at him, wiping rain from my eyes.

It may have been a full minute before he waved his hand for me to come into the breezeway, with his head turned up Hiller Street, as if he was and he wasn't beckoning to me. I didn't go right away. I stood against the damp, rough trunk of the tree and watched him through the rain and the roof runoff. When he gestured again I knew I had to go. I went because this was my home — time here, time there, this was my home, and the reason I'd worked my way back to Marion. I looked both ways, as if a car could come, and walked across the alley-sized street — thick, sandy mud in the rain — under the runoff curtain, and faced my great-grandfather.

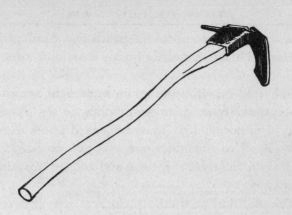

## CHAPTER SEVEN

# Joshua, the Captain, and John

YOU CAN SEE someone's picture in an album or on a wall and look at it hard over years until the image of that face is part of you but is a lie. A photograph is a moment, a slice the shutter cuts out of a second, and a person is all motion and time. Any one photograph would lie more about Joshua Carter than show the truth. The truth was that his face was a minor part of his expression: it was a long face fixed in a patient, slightly sad way around a drooping mustache and eyes that might belong to someone else living behind the face. But his expressions and speech were in his hands and head and shoulders. He talked quite a bit, yet he seldom said a word.

He looked up Hiller Street for some time, squinting occasionally as if he were trying to see something or understand it. Then he looked at me with his head off to one side, one eyebrow raised. He touched the material of his vest and nodded his chin toward me.

"Yes, sir, they're my only clothes." He nodded yes, and gestured with a tiny toss of his head up Hiller Street. "I sailed up from Cuttyhunk with Corbin Starkweather." He was still listening. "I left a steamer there, sir." Still listening; Tell me more, his look said. "I had some trouble with the cook." A raised eyebrow, a narrow look. "No, sir, I didn't do anything wrong." The eyes behind the face examined me, made some decision, and wandered away to my shorts and shirt.

But then they snapped back to my face and searched it for something else. My stomach caught itself and I was afraid. What was he looking for? A family resemblance or the signs of a liar? His look could be my first and toughest test.

"Mr. Carter, they tell me you build boats. I would like to learn to build boats. The way you build boats." Damn, a silent man can make talk sound foolish. "I need a job." What else was there to say?

His mouth drooped to fit his mustache, his eyes walked up the street, and his head shook, No, no, he didn't think so.

"I am not given to tobaccos, spirits, or degrading habits." It was a little desperate but it couldn't hurt.

Joshua Carter turned and walked back into the shop. In that moment I was panicked; my one plan had failed, I had backed off a cliff and was going to fall to the bottom. Just before he disappeared through the door, his hand came up behind him and gestured, Come on, then, he hadn't all day, come on. I almost tripped, trying to follow so quickly.

It was dark in the shop, and dry, and it was all wood. I mean it smelled like wood, sweet pine and bitter oak, and with the rain murmuring on the roof it sounded like wood. A head-high pile of wood shavings, scraps, and chips filled one end of the shop. The skeletons of two small boats hung upside down, end to end, propped from the floor and braced from the rafters. The rafters were crowded with tools and lumber. The windows looked out on the harbor, what I could see of it in the rain. A figure hunched over the counter that ran under the windows straightened up — though not all the way — and turned. Its voice boomed out, "Where in Christ's name did you get *that*?"

It was an old man's voice, loud out of any proportion to the hunched, white-haired old fellow who used it. Joshua Carter looked at me with just a little more pain and patience in his face and, eyes elsewhere, jerked his head toward the old man. Introduce yourself.

"Good afternoon," I said. "I am Jack Stone, sir."

"Fine, just fine. God *damn* but you're a sorry specimen. Joshua, you crack-brained half-wit, why in *hell* are you bringing this guttersnipe in here? *Look* at him. This wet wharf rat couldn't pour piss out of a boot with the directions on the heel. Hell's *bells,* just look at him. He'll *rust* anything he gets near."

Joshua handed me a broom and, with his hands and shoulders, said, The whole shop, but there was a broader shrug in the gesture that said, The whole place is a confusing mess, including this old rooster.

I took the broom and the old guy said, "*Jesus.* This isn't no Goddamned boardinghouse for Mongolian *morons.* You haven't got the *sense,* Josh, God gave an oyster. Je-*sus.*"

"Jack." Joshua finally spoke in a soft voice. "Please to meet my father, Captain Caleb Carter. Dad, let us show some encouragement to young Mr. Stone. He's only here to help for the afternoon." While he spoke, his eyes shifted nervously among the rafters; he did not like to speak and maybe I could see why.

"*Je*-sus, *Jo*-seph, and *Ma*-ry!" bellowed the Captain, and he followed it with a long string of obscenities. The Captain had certainly learned some colorful talk at sea. The tirade drove Joshua into his work, silently fitting the last ribs on one skeleton, and I quickly followed him away, sweeping at the end of the shop farthest from the Captain. Our retreat had no effect on the Captain's volume or his outrage. He dabbed the sweat from his face with a blue bandanna and went on for some time. A man who can swear that strong and that varied has got something to keep himself company.

I swept, as quickly and as well as I could, and I was saying to myself, All right, Jack, this is your one chance of making it here. But sweeping isn't fiddling; you can sweep only so well and no better. I swept and looked. I swept the benches and put the racks of auger bits in order. I swept under the benches between the chests of planes and markers and adzes and rivet bucks and mallets and I don't know what-all. They were all bright and sharp, ready to work. It came to me that they were still there in the boxes, all these tools, back home. Then it struck me that this was my home. . . . Was the home I knew far away right now being swept by my broom? Did height, width, and depth decide a place, or was time another depth or height that was part of a place? If I held a broom in my hand now in 1904, was it the same broom in 1981? Sure. How about an egg? Sure. No, it isn't, the egg becomes a chicken, maybe. Maybe the broom becomes splinters and dust. Maybe every place and every thing needs a time to be; maybe there's a dimension of being ticking inside every clock, inside every thing. What about me, then: if I was outside my own time, was I real? Yes, hell yes. I was real wherever I was, I carried reality with me. I kept sweeping. Maybe the world was real only if it was right now. I kept sweeping. I was here and I was real and I was sweeping.

How could I make them keep me?

The Captain had mostly quieted down and I was sweeping near Joshua, around his feet and behind him. When he was about to step back I'd move a little, then I'd go on. The place was not messy but it was dusty and full of chips. He was fitting ribs into the keel and it was careful work, the kind of fine detail that measurement starts and a sharp eye finishes. The ribs were oversized by a whisper so that Joshua could shave half a whisper away and press it into its notch with his powerful hands. One rib was two whispers over; Joshua wanted a chisel. On the bench behind me was a chest of chisels; he wanted the one inch and I handed it to him. He took it without looking and, with his flat, hard thumb as a guide and his other hand pushing, shaved away a delicate peel. He handed back the chisel as he fitted the rib; it was sized right but something in the notch caught it. The rib squeaked out and I could see a chip left in the notch that stopped the rib from seating. He would need another chisel, narrower, not the bevel-edged chisels from the chest's top row but one of the square-edged chisels, the half inch. I put it in his hand. He cut three ways — down, across, in — blew the chip out, and the rib pressed down into its place like it had grown there. I put the square-edged chisel back and we moved on to the next without realizing that we were working together.

Right here I've got to tell you something: about chisels I knew nothing; I don't believe I'd ever used one. Joshua had never spoken. He had looked up, he had stroked the rib's end, but I knew what he wanted. It wasn't telepathy, not magic, but familiarity that translated his nods and glances into needs. When Will and I worked on outboard motors or screen doors together we never spoke much, but we didn't have the need to speak. I was just beginning to recognize the shape of my father's silence in my great-grandfather; I was learning. Joshua's movements, his face, even the way his hands were built were familiar. They were, I guess, a family language. We set ten ribs together.

He picked up the last rib, hesitated, then stepped back and handed it to me. I nodded and tried it at its notch. Too wide but only by a sliver. I needed the beveled chisel, it appeared beside me, and, trying to use the same firm stroke I had watched Joshua's hands make, I coaxed a curl from the rib. It fit. Looser than his, but his shrug and eyebrows said, Good enough, good enough for beginners.

I swept around the boat skeletons. I found an oiled rag and wiped the chisels, closed the chest, and put the chest where it belonged. I *knew* where it belonged.

I knew the boy, too. I was almost finished, the shop looked clean. Little specks floated in the air and the rain drummed the roof. The Captain had muttered something about old bones and had followed Joshua into the house for tea. The boy walked in out of the rain with water streaming from his nose and chin and elbows and from the heavy coil of rope he carried across his shoulder. A puddle collected at his feet; his hair, brown like mine, black with the rain, was splayed out over his forehead.

"Hello?" he said to me. You could tell from the way he stood with that coil that he was strong, but agile too, a good runner, a tree climber, a swimmer.

"How old are you?" I asked him. It was a rude question. I did not mean it rudely, I was just not thinking too clearly.

He did not frown or bristle to have a stranger in his own house demanding answers. He liked the suddenness of it, I could tell. He smiled a big, open, toothy smile. "Fifteen," he said, "fifteen yesterday." Fifteen, like me. He was my grandfather, John Swain Carter. And here is the wonderful thing: I liked him immediately, and he liked me. We were already friends when I helped him take the coil of rope off his shoulders. "We'll have to hang that outside to dry tomorrow," he said.

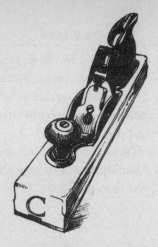

## CHAPTER EIGHT

# A Family

WE HUNG THE ROPE COIL on pegs in one of the storerooms along with other rope of many kinds. I had always wondered what those pegs were for. The storeroom smelled of tar and wax. We sat on kegs while he unlaced high leather shoes.

"Are you working here?" he asked, then grinned an apology. "I'm sorry. John Carter, glad to make your acquaintance."

"Jack Stone. Glad to meet you."

"I can't make out your accent, Jack." His was pure Cape Cod. "You're not Maine, you're not a

Newfie, not Marblehead or Boston. New York?"

"I guess you've got me," I said, thinking that television accents came from New York.

"Well? Are you working here? Where do you hail from? What brought you here?"

"I don't know whether I'm working here yet. I hope I am but I don't know. I came up to Cuttyhunk on a coaster and jumped ship because the cook knocked me around."

"Did you owe the boat any time?"

"No." I didn't know exactly what that meant but it didn't sound good.

"And what about the boatworks?"

"I came up with Corbin Starkweather."

"Nice fellah. Our boat."

"A Carter boat? The *Allise?* Yes, nice fellow. I walked in off the street, or, really, your father brought me in out of the rain."

"Well, he likes you if he left you in here alone. I guess you've met" — he put his arms up like a bear and lowered his voice — "Captain Bones?"

"Good grief, yes. He thought I was the next worse thing to a garden slug. He said my mother was a Spanish burro and my father was something like a Gibraltar ape."

"Did he call you a wrecker?"

"No."

"Or a lawyer?"

"No."

"How about a sealer?"

"No, not that either."

He shrugged. "Don't worry, then. You fall in with the rest of us and no lower. Above wreckers, lawyers, and sealers, below Mrs. Taber."

"He has a lady friend?"

"No, no." He laughed. "A lady in the town he thinks of as quite refeened."

"Refeened?"

"A refined, high-toned sort takes the Captain's admiration every time."

"Is he as mean as he sounds?"

"His bark is worse than his bite, for the most part, but he can be as tough as leather when he wants to be. Mother has his number and he is as gentle as a new lamb around her. But get his dander up and that's a barn fight. A few years ago, ninety-eight it was, and the Captain — who was all of eighty — saw some young Boston city dude whipping his horse right up here on Front Street. The Captain jerked him down off his cart and knocked the stuffing out of him. A real ripper when he's riled. There!" He took off his boots and stood up. "I'll stuff these with rags and they'll be dry tomorrow afternoon."

"Is he a sea captain?"

"Is he? Why, Caleb commanded an ironclad in the war."

"The Civil War?"

He looked at me, puzzled. "What war did you think? Of course."

"Of course," I said.

"Are you feeling well?"

"Tired." And I was. I looked around in the storeroom and wondered if they would let me sleep there for the night. I was winding down and had no place to go, though I was in my own home.

There was a whistle, a high-low-high-low whistle like a short bugle call. Someone was whistling for a dog or for children. John started out the door. "Come on," he said. "That's suppertime."

"Well, I haven't been —"

"Oh, come on. You've been, now." He looked back at me, at my shorts and tennis shirt. "That's the strangest get-up, Jack. No offense meant, but what else did they wear on that schooner of yours?" I could only smile and shrug. "Well, come along or the Captain will have you for supper. But let's go through my room first."

We went through the shop and ran up the back stairs and down the hall to the corner room, my room, except it was John's room now. My own bed was even there too, with the trundle under it and the turned bedposts, but in John's room manila rope woven in and out of the rope leads held the mattress in the frame, not plywood. John shucked his wet

clothes into a pile and toweled off. He opened the
cupboard that's built over the stairs and tossed out
bib overalls and flannel shirts and light wool socks.
"Hurry," he said.

"I'm sorry?"

"Put them on, hurry. She'll whistle again in a
minute and then the Captain will be wrung for fair."

"Really, John, I can wear my own and eat outside
in —"

"Hustle, Jack, let's get down there." He had his
half on.

I took off my clothes and put on the things he
offered. New washed, they felt soft and scratchy and
warm and cool at the same time. Somehow I became
even more weary in them. He gathered our damp
things together and we tumbled down the stairs to
the kitchen.

Of that whole evening, I remember most Minnie
Carter's face and hands. I do not remember much
else, really. She had a warm, wide face, full of smile
and eyes; a slow and peaceful face that settled on
John like sun on a field, gladly. She reached out and
rubbed his cheek and smoothed his hair. "You'll be
Jack, then," she said to me, and I felt warmed, too.

"Jack Stone, I'd have you meet my mother, Mrs.
Minnie Carter."

I bowed, awkwardly, for I'd never bowed before,
and said, "I'm very happy to meet you, Mrs. Carter,

and I hope I am not inconveniencing or intruding. I do not mean to impose myself on you." I was as worn out as a back-door mat but I was still trying my best. Those brown, kind eyes seemed to know that, and appreciate the thought, but they worried for me at the same time. She was a woman with a talent for caring.

"Minnie." It was the Captain, already seated at the head of the table. "Perhaps *Mr.* Stone can speechify *after* victuals."

"Captain Carter," she said, "you are, as usual, correct: it is time for us all to eat. Let us join you." He inclined his head to her. John was right: she had his number. John held her chair at the end of the table opposite the Captain. I stood across from Joshua, I remember that. I don't remember sitting down but I remember her serving chowder in bowls, opening the napkin over a basket of steaming biscuits. I remember the smells, her hands, some of the taste. The next thing I remember is John helping me up the stairs, the trundle bed, and I remember even a few tears, relief, so tired, home, safe, sorry, sleep.

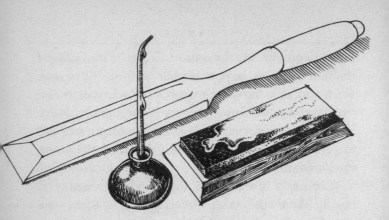

## CHAPTER NINE

# A Chelsea Clock

SOME WOOD is bitter, some wood is sweet. But there's no sweeter wood than cedar. It's light when you heft a plank onto the workbench, and it's soft enough so you can groove it with your thumbnail. The burred marks of the sawblade, just as it came out of the water mill in Rochester, give its face a fuzzy texture. You back it against stops on the bench and you are ready to work it smooth. You use a jack plane for this work, a hefty fifteen inches long, and before you start you hold it upside down and lengthwise against the light to check the depth and squareness of the cutter; what the Captain would call the set and truth of the iron. Then you can begin, feet apart, hands ready to listen to the wood through the knob and swell of the plane. Long sweeps, sure and even-pressured, catching only the ridges at first. More sweeps that shave off the crests and open the cedar's heart, a smooth gleaming of regular grain surrounded by the dull, weathered rough, like the heart of a warm jewel, but fragrant. The full spice scent curls out of cedar and closes around your head and shoulders as the shavings curl off the new surface and close around your feet with a dry rustle.

There was a clock in the shop, hung on the wall, and it was wound every seven days. I had seen it wound twice, now. The clock had a pacing sound, unhurried and businesslike. It rang the watch bells, a little event every half hour. I was smoothing a whole stack of planks, work the Captain himself had taught me. Gruff, bad-mouthing, impatient if you listened only to his words, but if you watched his hands, calm and helpful, you got another message. He would not snatch the plane away like someone who couldn't stand watching a beginner screw up. He could watch me screw up all day, it seemed, and his mouth going all the time, though he would put his hands over mine and show me the corrections. I learned from him.

There were so many planks to do that I didn't concern myself with rushing. I just laid both surfaces smooth and as flat as I could, and while that clock walked on and over my thoughts, I began thinking about the way time is built.

It must be ordered or put together some way, right? And if I had turned up in 1904 it had to be . . . flexible, loose, changeable, at least in ways or maybe places. The curls of cedar came off, spiraled up and out of the plane, and the clock ticked. It rang two and two, four bells, two o'clock.

Ticks added up to bells, eight bells to a watch of four hours, six watches made a day, seven days a week, about thirty a month, or three hundred and sixty-five a year. Straight time, straight and flat like the plank I'd just finished.

I hefted up a new plank and checked the set and truth of the iron again. I began again. No, time wouldn't begin again like planks laid end to end; the parts of it would be parts of nature: days, yes, but not weeks; moon months, sure, but not thirty days hath September; years, yes, if a year meant a circle around the sun.

Circles, round, time going round. The face of the clock was marked with Roman numerals. I knew why now, because we marked boat ribs and parts in the same way: all the numerals could be struck with a straight chisel. Nothing straight in time, though:

round. The clockface was lettered CHELSEA, MASS'TS, and the hands swung round and past the same place they'd been an hour before, or this morning, or last night. Yes, time was like a clock, whirling about. I had been whirled off one clockface and onto — no, it didn't work that way. I turned the plank over and began that side.

No, the clock idea only allowed reliving the same face over. Time would start and start again every time the hand came around. No.

I ran the plane halfway down the plank. It was fair, now, and my hands were beginning to learn the even pressure that peeled away a single long curl of — a round curl, a spiral, a whirl. I stopped. I picked up the curl and held it. I made a groove with my thumbnail across the rolled top and, holding the inside end and the outside end, pulled out the curl to make a long spiral, a helix. The thumbnail grooves matched all the way up, tier by tier. I bent the helix this way and that. I could make one curl touch another, it happened naturally. Was I looking at a model of time?

No, not a good model, but I began to understand, now, how it *could* have happened. How whirling, repeating, but not recurring, time could bend and touch. If music had dimensions of pitch and beat and length, then time could have its own dimensions, its own height and width and direction. If it did, could it bend toward itself too closely? If it did, could it have thin spots? Could it buckle like a bridge or fold like a fan or storm like a sky? Could it be that at a certain time, at some certain place, I had been in a time storm, a storm without rain?

I looked at the spiraling wood chip until I heard the Captain bawling at the coal- and icehouse gang. I put it into my pocket and finished planing that side, too. I was getting good at smoothing. It was work that let you think.

I saw how it might happen but too much was missing. The planks had dimensions I could feel. Music was something I could hear. But I could not put a measure to time. It seemed that time had its own measures that ignored me, everyone. I had never thought of time as a material, like cedar or canvas or clay. It could be, I began to suspect, very like this cedar: you used it, shaped what you had to what you could make of it. I had always thought of time as rigid, locked, tamperproof. But even if you don't get shunted backward half a hundred years, you can feel the differences in its texture: time on a rainy Sunday morning was not the same as time in the middle of a math test. Time had a grain, like the cedar, and it was a long, one-way grain.

The Captain was back. "Jack Stone, it would take three or maybe four lazy Lascars, all working in concert, to be as slow as you on a fast day." You see, even the Captain knew time was fast and slow. "Are you planing those planks with a spokeshave? *Je*-sus, *Jo*-seph, and *Ma*-ry can you go no faster? Can you not make a day see profit?"

"I'm planing extra smooth for you, Captain. I know you like a good job and despise a careless workman." I was learning from Minnie how to get around behind the Captain, and, beside that, he was in a good mood. His shouts and threats had a light air, that day.

"Still, Jack, still." He moved down the bench to Skiff One, as we called it, which was nearly planked up. Skiff Two was ribbed out and had braces and knees laid in. Things moved amazingly quickly; we had no power tools (we had no power), but the tools we had were just right for their purpose. You pick up an electric drill in any hardware and it's an amazing machine, but it's designed to do almost anything: bore big holes and little holes, buff cars, sand chairs, stir paint, and it's pretty good at all of those. We had no one tool that could do all those jobs, but we had dozens of tools, each with one narrow purpose, and it did that one thing as well as it could be done. We had a contraption the size of a fat baby that did nothing but bore holes in decks; before you could adjust your Black and Decker wonder and run your extension cord and choose your bit and line it all up, we could fetch the deck drill and sink four or five holes as clean and straight as a sunbeam.

Another thing: our tools were sharp. I don't mean we had three sharp chisels among all the tools and I don't mean pocketknife sharp. I mean that every chisel, wood bit, drawknife, marking gauge, and plane iron, everything was sharp enough to shave hair off an egg, scary sharp.

*Our* tools. I'm making it sound like I was building Skiff Two by myself. I wasn't, but I was helping. The Captain and Joshua knew more about putting tools to wood than anyone in Massachusetts today, and even young John, who the Captain said couldn't butcher a toothpick out of a timber raft, would stand up as a respectable cabinetmaker. I was learning. If I point to the sharpness of our tools, it is because sharpening the tools was part of my job and all three of those craftsmen showed me the importance of a keen edge. Through the day I brought down and whetted the little blades of wood-boring bits, the flat slicing edges of chisels and plane irons, the curves of gouges, and the burrs of scrapers. I was proud to see them work for skillful hands. I was proud to work with that skill, to be part of this family. It was a piece of wry luck.

"Jack, can you help me out here on fifty-four?" John was caulking deck seams on a catboat outside. For us they had numbers, since the owner selected his own name.

"Captain?" I asked.

"Go, git, gone!" He groused, "You two are like barnyard hens and do about as much."

"What's up?"

"Climb up here, Jack, and hold this go-devil for the seams in this cockpit sole."

The soft ropes of cotton caulking were laid out beside the fore and aft cracks. "You need a go-devil for this?" It was a big, dull-bladed iron with a two-handed handle that forced the cotton in between the planking where it would swell up watertight.

"Well, it's four quarters stock and, shoot, Jack," — he lowered his voice — "I just wanted the company. Let's get this done and go swimming."

"Any blues run tonight?"

He looked at the harbor. "They're there. Those little sweet tinker blues and those big rogue blues as would eat your favored foot, given the opportunity."

"And opportunity knocks . . ." I said, holding the go-devil and a string of caulk into a seam.

"But . . . *once, twice, thrice.*" He pounded the string in as I walked the blade along.

"Foul hook . . . some . . . pogeys?" I asked between blows.

"Possible . . . possible . . . sooner . . . troll some . . . feather bucks . . . better . . . sport."

I moved the devil onto the next seam. "Hell with sport. Get fish, think about sport while we're eating."

"Good . . . plan. . . ." We started again. "Get this . . . puppy . . . done."

We were sweating and joking in the cockpit, pounding away, when — between blows — I glanced through the little square tiller hole in the transom and saw, coming toward us, the scowling, slack-eyed face of One-armed Higgins.

"Jack!" John shouted just as the mallet hit me, glancing off my left hand and sending a bolt of pain up my arm. I'd jerked the go-devil to one side trying to get up, get away, and though he'd tried to pull it, John had caught me with the mallet. I only had a few seconds, and frantically looked toward the hole; someone was coming up the ladder. I threw the go-devil forward through the companionway and scrambled after it into the cabin.

John knelt in the cockpit, still holding the mallet. Holding my hand and trying not to cry out, I saw him look up quickly and heard Higgins's voice. Higgins was drunk.

"What hell's the goddamn commotion? What the hell? What?"

John looked at me, still puzzled. I shook my head desperately: Don't let him see me, John, don't let him aboard.

"Boy? You going to talk to me? By Christ I'll . . ."

"Higgins." The Captain's voice. It was a formal

tone but seemed as loud as a shout. It was probably a way of speaking you need on the quarterdeck of an ironclad. It stopped Higgins. "If you have business here you may approach me and leave my help to their work. Well?"

I could see Higgins's one hand. It tightened on the cockpit coaming and the ladder creaked as he shifted toward the Captain. "It's my goddamn boat, that wormy crackerbox you threw together. It's drawing in the water. What you going to do? About the boat? You going to fix the sonofbitch? Goddamn —"

"Higgins, this is *my* cove and *I* will do the blaspheming here. As for your boat, I am little surprised she leaks. You have neglected an excellent piece of our work, have soaked the deck in blood, have allowed fresh water to sit in her, and you have not painted her for five years. She has returned good service for poor treatment."

"She's going to be fixed. You're going to fix her."

"I will fix your boat, Mr. Higgins."

"You damn bet you fix her. Your mistakes. Drawing in the water."

"I will refit your boat for one-third its original price."

"You'll go straight to hell."

"I have no doubt, Mr. Higgins, but this is a fair

price." With customers, even with this drunk and insulting intruder, the Captain was as proper as a church deacon.

The hand fumbled on the coaming. "Just caulk the bastard up, then."

"No."

"I'm telling you to caulk her so she'll float!"

"She deserves better than that. Half a job will kill her. Burn her, if you wish, but if she's to float she will do it well. No one else in this town will touch her. She is ours. Do you have the cash?"

"I've got the peel, Carter."

"Then when will you bring her in?"

"New cordage."

"Naturally."

"Sails."

"You'll have to see Sperry Sails about that."

"Christ."

"When, Mr. Higgins? I must schedule time."

"Monday."

"Wednesday a week."

"Too long! My ass is wet."

"You have neglected her long enough to endure ten days' discomfort. Bail. Good day, sir."

"Bah!" The hand disappeared, the ladder banged the hull in three steps, and we heard him lurch away unevenly, cursing to himself.

In a few moments the ladder was gently repositioned and the Captain's hands appeared on the rail. My own hand was pulsing with a deep ache and a sting. "Where's Jack?"

"He's in the cabin getting the iron." John looked back at me. "I dropped it in." He was still confused.

"You boys move fifty-four, here, over, and piece up a cradle for one-eighteen. Her model is hanging over the onion bin."

"Are we going to do work for Higgins?" John asked. "He's a rummy."

"Yes. He is also a superb waterman, a first-rate naturalist, and there is only one better wingshot on the bay. When he was your age he could —" He stopped. A moment later the hands disappeared abruptly. The Captain started down the ladder but stopped at the bottom. His voice came over the side, smaller now: "Disaster dogs some men and bites at them wherever they rest. Some men thrive on it, but they are often dangerous men. Some men wait it out and go on. Some it poisons and they begin to suspect it always will and run with the dogs that pursued them. Even the best. John?"

"Yes, Grandfather."

"You know the *Wanderer?* The wreck on Naushon Shore?"

"Yes, Grandfather."

"Look at it every time and tell yourself you will handle your boat in a better way because of it. Look at Bernard Higgins every time and tell yourself that you don't really know him or what he's seen."

He went away, then. I had the idea that the crews of his ironclads must have hated him and loved him and served him without question, with a will. Also, that holding men by your will is an effort, a struggle you might give up gladly after a life at sea, because the Captain, by the time he had reached Skiff One inside, was singing a fairly interesting chantey about island maidens and navy men.

I could hold out no longer. I began to whimper, and the frightened, hurt tears I had blinked away were followed by a rush of crying, relief, and pain. John climbed down into the cabin with me and carefully took my swelling hand.

"Mother will look at this right off," he said, "but there's something else wrong. What happened, there? You and Higgins. Tell me. I can help."

I don't know why we were so close, John and I. Maybe because we were family, and knew each other's ways; maybe because we were just us; but in two weeks John Swain Carter had become my best friend. I will never have another friend like him. I could share anything with him. Even this. I snuffled to a stop. My nose was running.

"John, I've got some things to tell you. Hard things to tell."

"Jack, I don't care what you've done, you didn't

do it with a cruel thought in your brain. Is it some mistake? Some shame? I cannot think bad of you. Tell me."

"I wish it were just shame. It would be easier, I swear." I laughed a little with tears still coming. "It's harder than that. Not here and not now, though. Later. Can you trust me?"

"What do you think? Come on now. Mother will want to get at that hand."

## CHAPTER TEN

# Conspirators

IT WAS MONDAY, so we knew Minnie was in the wash yard. John and I came around the spar shed and she was hanging sheets, laughing with Joshua. When we appeared she beamed at us over the washline like a girl, but Joshua fell silent. He blushed and left murmuring about something in the lumber sheds. He was a very private man.

She was not private in the same way. Her happiness flowed out, and her concern, too, as her smile changed. "Jack, what's happened to you? My poor dear, you've hurt yourself. John, how did it happen?

Come over here, lamb." She was cradling my hand in hers, fingers moving softly over the bones. "Our dear boy, my, my, my." She clucked and made pained noises as she turned the hand and forearm gently.

When you're fifteen you're supposed to be tough, I know. Minnie made me feel it was all right if I wasn't a paratrooper. I was glad she wanted to baby me. There are worse things when your hand feels like an oversmoked ham.

"Minnie!"

"Wash yard, Captain Carter."

"Minnie!"

"Here we are. Now, Jack, I don't think anything is broken, but that doesn't mean it won't hurt for a few days."

"Here you are! You two are on the dog cart again while I am working like a coolie."

"You were ever a fierce worker, Captain."

"Yes, well, yes. It's in my bones to put in an honest day's labor, but these boys —"

"Captain, these boys profit by your example every day. I see it in them. But look at poor Jack, here, he's got himself a proud hand and a deep bruise in your service."

"Spit on it! Spit on it! That's what I told them off Norfolk Roads when limbs was getting snipped off like okra at picking time. Spit on it, I'd tell them, and I'd see a gunner sluice down the stump end of an arm — excuse me, Minnie — with hot tar and keep laying his gun."

"They were iron men, Captain." I tell you Minnie had that man and was driving him like a carriage.

"I'll tell you they were iron men. They could stick it. Now these lazy —"

"These boys are fine boys and look up to you as an example. I am going to ask you a little favor, Captain."

"Why, of course, Minnie." He was all courtly, now, an officer and a gentleman attending on a lady's wishes.

"I need some errands run around and across the harbor. Now I know your work load is strenuous —"

"Do not consider it."

"However, I would like to use the boys for a few hours."

"Of course, Minnie, of course." The Captain turned to us and gave us our orders. "You carry out Mrs. Carter's errands smartly, hear? Mind your manners and act in a way becoming to Mrs. Carter. Understood?"

"Yes, sir," we both said, but we did not salute.

"Carry on, then. Well, Minnie, I'll bid you a good day. I've a busy schedule." He walked out of the wash yard with the bearing of a king — or that of a captain of ironclads. It was true that Minnie flattered him and defused much of his anger, but it was flattery she believed, and the result gave the old man the best part of his youth back. It was an exchange of love, which was not so unusual in this household, for that was Minnie's talent.

In the kitchen Minnie washed my hand and bandaged it in clean rags, with an herb-smelling packing against the skin. "This poultice will draw the humors," she said. It sounded like mumbo jumbo to me but I didn't think it could hurt and, really, it felt sort of cozy.

"A pound of butter, five pounds of flour, two of leaf lard, one pound of raisins, two of white beans, a quart of molasses." She spoke her list without hesitation and then said, "John?" He repeated her list almost perfectly and she reminded him of the soda and he said, "Yes, ma'am." It made me realize how sharp memories can be. Paper was expensive, and it was used carefully, not for everyday lists and reminders. They trusted their memories and, like muscles, their memories were strong from use. Joshua and the Captain kept tables of figures and a world of measurements in their heads. Both knew all the dimensions of each boat they had built, as the Captain had known the number of Higgins's boat when he asked John to build a cradle for it. Minnie had no cookbooks and seldom, that I saw, referred to the recipe cards she kept in a kitchen drawer. There was a tide table pinned to the shop wall but it was consulted only once or twice a week.

"On your way back, go through the chicken house and bring the eggs. And make certain Jack doesn't use his hand carrying groceries."

"Yes, ma'am."

It is difficult to say whether the tide chart got so few glances because of good memories or because their senses were so keen and tuned to their world. On our way up Hiller Street even I could tell it was coming onto low tide by the smell, the pleasantly overrich muskiness of the harbor's edge ooze. Listening, too: I could hear gulls keening and squabbling in the mud beside the hard-sounding stone wharf. All this came through other sounds and smells: the Bigelows' stable, the chicken yard, the tar and canvas smell of Sperry's sail loft, and the faint, not unpleasant smell of the privies.

In case you're wondering, we had paper in the privy but it wasn't on a roll and it wasn't the soft, fluffy kind of paper you use. It came in thin, slick-surfaced sheets in a flat box, and the first time I tried to use it I thought it was just ridiculous. Bathroom habits (I mean privy habits really) were far different, though. The Carters weren't so fussy about being alone, for one thing: "obeying the call of nature," as the men put it, was considered a natural sort of function and our privy was a two-holer. I learned by watching Joshua how to crumple the slick paper and use it as a fine-surfaced ball. Minnie had her own single-seat compartment entered through the other side of the privy, somewhat better finished out with a smooth carved seat and a curtain up high. Her door had a crescent moon cutout and ours had a sun cutout, which was a standard way of distinguishing female and male privies and maybe other things. It was not the green-tiled bathroom I was used to.

You would have liked the general store. It smelled like the inside of some foreign spice cake. That was from the barrels of fresh and dried fruit, the bins of tea and the scarlet coffee grinder flecked with dark brown dust, the hanging strings of dried figs and onions, glass jars of glazed fruit . . . strong smells of distant places. The meat counter was not glass and porcelain, and next to a supermarket cooler it might appear grisly: it was an elm chopping block and a maple counter with three or four chickens and some large cloth-wrapped cuts of beef and mutton. There was blood and, at one end of the counter, a pile of bones covered with cloth. The cloth was protection against the flies that buzzed and fussed everywhere. There were wheels of cheese, too, though we ordered ours from the farmer who drove milk and cream and butter and eggs through Marion in the cool early morning, around seven o'clock, before the heat of the day would spoil his goods.

Mr. Olsen made our order up. Again, paper wasn't a cheap throwaway. The trip to the store was as bulky as the trip back because we brought the cloth sacks, tins, and wooden pails to carry home most of our purchases and all of it went in a wide shopping basket. There's sense in that. Baskets were important tools: they held and organized and carried all kinds of shop and house items. They were light and strong and most of them were open-woven so they breathed, which is good for storing vegetables or holding wet clothes. There were a dozen basket materials and constructions in many sizes. There was sense in them, too. In fact, I saw a lot of sense in those days. It made me guilty, at times, because it seemed to me that my time had come to use oil and money as substitutes for sense and planning.

I saw a lot of sense but I saw some other things, too. I saw some mumbo jumbo and some superstition: if a bird flew into the house it meant someone was going to die; you took a slice of bread with a crust still on your plate, someone would go hungry; the wind set a rocking chair going, the dead were crying against a wrong. People believed these things. I saw some foolishness: there was a slightly crazy way everyone talked about the brave glory and noble sacrifice of war, the most recent being the Spanish-American. Sentimentality: every mother was a saint, every child was an Angel of Heaven — damn, it was enough to make Doris sound as cold as a tax lawyer.

I saw some cruelty, mostly to horses worked too hard on hot days, even though only stupid people did that, and then mostly with livery horses or animals that belonged to their employers. Some horses died, though, and it wasn't unusual to see a wagon go by hauling a dead horse to the tanners and renderers in New Bedford, with the hauling horses nervous and prancy from the smell of horse death.

I saw a lot of prejudice. I can't explain why, but all those people had it in for the Italians and the Irish as a lower, less clean and honest and godly sort of people. The Portuguese fishermen and their families were even lower, and black people were beneath them all, but they were excused because that was "only their nature."

I saw a lot of religion, a lot of churchgoing people who held tight to their beliefs and never questioned them. Or anything else involving God. Faith was the article you wanted. If you got too near questioning, say, whether the Red Sea truly did part, the rest of the congregation would gather around to help as they did when one of your family was sick, because "your faith was slipping."

We went through the chicken house on the way back and brought seven eggs into the kitchen.

It seems to me now that I saw a lot of practical sense and not a lot of emotional sense. Chicken houses, baskets, tools, boats — they were worked out in an admirable way to conserve the time and effort of people who didn't have many sources of cheap power. Religion, racism, superstition — they weren't worked out because they weren't questioned and revised and requestioned the way a sail plan or a deck boring tool would be. Faith was too strong and too comforting. Or maybe life was enough harder that the practical business of making your way in the world needed all the attention you could spare, and you stacked the religion and emotion and all in the corner, dusty and unquestioned, just so you wouldn't burn your mind out.

Thinking it over I see that we've changed some, but we still take our religion blindly, especially around Christmas. As for superstition, I know plenty of people who can't exactly tell you what vitamin C does but they choke down two or three pills the size of quail eggs every morning. You think about it.

Minnie looked at my hand again and loosened the

bandage. "It will swell some, still, but don't pay it heed, lamb. You boys take this basket to Mrs. Hammett, this one to Mrs. Saltonstall, and take these things to Mr. Pickett at the lighthouse."

"Yes, ma'am," John said, and he seemed flushed.

"You take your time and, Jack, don't strain that hand. Try not to use it at all. You look out for him, John. There are two slices of pie for you boys in Mr. Pickett's hamper." Minnie's pies were like a whole dinner between crusts. I can taste them even now. "Skate on out of here, you boys, and try to catch something for supper." She walked us out to the door with her arms through ours.

We were halfway down to the float when Minnie called, "Say hello to Ruth for me, John."

Once again John blushed, even redder, and didn't answer. I shouted back, "We'll bring home some blues, Minnie!" She waved and went back inside. I was excited; I didn't even notice my hand. "Come, John, let's get those blues. Let's drag in a bluefish big enough shut the Captain up. What do you say?"

"No reason why not, I suppose."

"Come on, John, what's got into you all of a sudden?"

"Okay, Jack. Let's murder some bluefish."

*Captain Gnat* was John's boat, built as a gift from Joshua on his eleventh birthday and named, in fun, for a friend of Joshua's in Bristol, Rhode Island:

Captain Nathaniel Herreshoff, the yacht designer.

"You want these back here under the seat?"

"Hell, no, Jack!" He was getting his composure back again. "Put all the baskets forward and cover them up. Then get the mast stepped."

She was swampscott sailing dory, the kind we sold for about sixty-five dollars with oars and sails.

"Take the spring in, lubber. For a schooner boy you are surely a green hand. Or is that what you really did?" He was himself again, grinning and kidding, but serious under it. I knew I would tell him how I really came to this Marion, and it wasn't just because of my promise to tell him. I wanted badly to share the burden of it. Right now, though, I wanted to sail.

"Do you want to fool around with springs and signals and piping you aboard, or do you want to sail, John Carter?"

"Cast off, lubber," he said, and I did. The wind filled the spritsail, *Captain Gnat*'s weather gunwale swung up, John let the centerboard drop, and we slid away from the float with a whisper, a gurgle, and then, as we came up to speed, the four-knot hiss of bubbles breaking out from under the stern. Off through the anchorage we skimmed, slewing close around the transoms of moored boats and pinching up into the wind above bows and mooring lines, almost not clearing them, tense and trying to make the boat go with the soles of our feet and — every time — swinging around clear with a hoot of laughter and ready for the next contest.

We ate Minnie's pie right off. Didn't even get across the harbor. We swooped downwind to the rocky mouth of Hammett's Cove and got the sail off her so we could row in. We tied up to a little cypress tree on Hammett's front lawn and gave Mrs. Hammett her basket of herbs and preserves (Minnie needn't have sent it. I'm sure it was just her excuse to get us out of the shop, but it was her way to do good on both ends). Mrs. Hammett gave us slices of pie, too, and we ate them, leaning on our oars about three strokes from the cypress. Just for the sake of comparison, you understand.

"Whose is better, John?"

"Minnie has the edge, I think."

"To really tell I'd have to sample again, though."

We rowed up the eastern shore of the harbor as our next stop was only half a mile, and to windward. As we tied up at the Saltonstall float, John looked a little tight around the mouth and missed the cleat with his last hitch twice. "Damnation!" he said, very soft but fervent. It was a curious day for old John.

We came up a long lawn walk to a house the size of a small hotel. Not so small, really, and with a red tile roof. It's still there, they built her solid. I'd seen the house in my own time, sitting big and handsome across the harbor. I wasn't thinking that much about it — to tell you the truth I was wondering what kind of pies Mrs. Saltonstall put out — but the feeling was there and it set me up in an odd way for what happened then: Ruth Saltonstall opened the door.

I've got to stop here. Mainly because it embarrasses me to talk about it, partly because . . . well, I've got to stop, here.

## CHAPTER ELEVEN

# Ruth

I'LL TELL YOU the truth, I get all flustered talking about Ruth Saltonstall. I was flustered then, when she opened the door. It was chiefly the eyes, I think, gray eyes with a snap, a steady look that was intense but not intimidating, eyes ready to see everything. Her face was strong but warm, because of a full underlip beneath a wide, quiet mouth. Her cheeks were high and smooth, with a fleck, the smallest flaw in her right cheek, a tiny scar. It gave her whole face a softness. It made you want to touch her cheek.

Much later it was her smile, the way she would snort when I made a bad pun, the way her hands looked tying a knot or holding a tiller or just handing me a cup, but as she stood in the doorway it was her eyes and that mouth and the tiny fleck adorning her cheek. I was staring. I hope that I at least had my mouth closed.

Her eyes turned to John. "Your boat isn't in sailing shape?"

It was clear why John had been blushing with Minnie. His ears were as red as tomato slices. He looked down at the porch and he felt a sprung nail head with his toe. "No, no, she's in good shape."

"The blues aren't running?"

"No, Ruth, the blues are all over the place, I hear tell."

"You lost your handlines."

"No, they're right . . . well, you know where they are."

"I do. So why haven't you come to take me fishing?"

"It's only that . . . well, Ruth . . ." The nail head was becoming more fascinating.

"Haven't we been pulling in bluefish and striper together for six years?"

"Sure. We have. But . . . well, it's been busy at the boatworks and we're getting that catboat and the two skiffs out and —"

"I'm waiting." Oh, she was angry with John, and it only made her eyes snap brighter and her face glow. I knew that I would take her fishing every day, if she would let me, and I would build the boat and tow it with my teeth, if I had to, singing "The Star Spangled Banner" around the rope, if it was necessary, into a forty-knot breeze, if that was required, and I would break through the ice in the winter, if she wanted.

"Look here, Ruth, a couple of weeks ago I sailed over here right into the middle of that garden party and came near knocking over the teapot on that one fella, that Richard Crocker, and *Moses*, Ruth, the way I figured, you didn't want me stumbling around all the proper goings-on over here dripping fish gurry on the doilies. Well, that was my figuring."

"John Swain Carter—" She stopped, exasperated, that handsome mouth set tight. She looked at me and I grinned back at her like a dog waiting for table scraps. She frowned and turned back. "John Carter, you are the perfect fool."

He laughed softly and stomped at the nail head as if it were an ant. "Yes, Ruth."

"I expect you to slide over here tomorrow morning and I expect us to hook some fish for breakfast."

He seemed relieved that she was angry with him for neglecting her.

"I'll see he makes it in good time, miss," I said.

"Excuse me, Jack." He finally looked up. "I'd like you to meet Miss Ruth Borden Saltonstall. Miss Saltonstall, this is Jack Stone, my friend and a new apprentice at the boatworks. Jack joined us a few weeks ago."

"Glad to make your aquaintance, Mr. Stone. Of the Marblehead Stones?"

"No, miss, of the, ah, New York Stones. You have a delightful homesite, Miss Saltonstall." I was trying to keep her talking. She had to think I was charming and bright. If she didn't think so, I would be obliged to go back to the boatworks and use the deck borer on my head. "The maples and elms must be beautiful in the autumn." They were in the Marion I had come from.

"Why yes, Mr. Stone. You have a good eye for these things. I hope we may bring Mr. Stone with us, John."

"Of course. We are seldom apart nowadays, Jack and I."

"Mr. Stone, John and I have been fishing friends since we were children."

"As I gather, Miss Saltonstall, though I did not mean to eavesdrop."

She laughed and her mouth was soft again. We laughed with her and John was happier but still blushing. Just being near her, I guess. I, myself, was completely at ease and the very model of suave decorum, though I did manage to back off the porch just then and fall into a large pyrocanthus bush. It's difficult to make out that you did a thing like that on purpose. As I struggled to get my feet out of the branches and onto solid ground, John was laughing so hard he had to put down the basket, and Ruth was leaning against the doorjamb. I looked up at them and said, "You've got a fine gardener, too, Miss Saltonstall. I've just been looking at his work."

They laughed even harder, and I got to laughing, and we were all sitting on the porch steps giggling and talking, and I've almost never been as happy.

"We've got to catch the last of the breeze, Jack," John said, looking out to the outer harbor and the lighthouse.

"You two clowns catch your breeze and I'll see you both in the morning." We stood up.

"I am delighted to meet you, Miss Saltonstall," I said.

"Seeing that you approve of my gardener, Mr. Stone, I think it would be seemly for you to call me Ruth."

"Thank you, Ruth. Someone here is a wonderful gardener. Everything here is fresh and blooming, including you."

"My gracious, will you listen to him, John? How

does he get anything done at the boatworks, while he's thinking of flowery things to say? We have a curious new partner, John."

"It is curious," John said with half a smile, "for at work he is remarkably ignorant, down to forgetting dates and even the President's name."

"He sounds pretty, though. You teach our John some charming things to use on the ladies of this town."

"Yes, ma'am," I replied, "but he is a poor study. He has his head buried in the wood chips most of the time."

"I know. He is hopeless. Both of you are. Go catch your breeze."

We were halfway down the walk when I remembered that we had not given her the basket. I was carrying it away with us. "Be right back!" I shouted to John, and ran up the walk. She was still sitting on the porch.

"Miss Saltonstall . . ."

"Ruth."

"Yes, ma'am . . . yes, Ruth. This is from Mrs. Carter for Mrs. Saltonstall."

She took it and put in on the step beside her. "Please thank Mrs. Carter for us." She watched me with her gray eyes, bold and unmoving, as though she knew I wanted to say something more.

"Ruth . . ."

"Yes?"

"May I . . . see you, may I call on your some-time?"

"Mr. Stone, you are a very forward young man. Of course not." But her face was not unpleased. I tried to keep my own face from falling and stayed a moment longer. "However," she said, "I look forward to the time when you return for Mrs. Carter's basket."

I tried not to whoop out of pure glee. I trusted myself to a few words — Thank you, Apologies for being too bold, See you tomorrow — but I was grinning very broadly and I made it only a few steps down the path before I broke into a run. Down the lawn I hopped and turned and waved to her. She waved back.

It's easy to see a lot of girls on Silvershell Beach in the summer, and to see a lot of each girl as she soaks up the rays in her bikini, but you take a truly beautiful girl in a long, white linen dress with puffy sleeves and very plain but elegant in a swaying sort of way, the white showing off the color of her skin — the color of light baked bread — with her long hair piled up . . . why, Silvershell in a heat wave never had anything as attractive and exciting as Ruth Saltonstall sitting on those porch steps.

John had stepped the mast and had cast off, tack-ing back and forth a little way out. As I pounded down onto the float, he shot up and came about right beside it. "Come on, Jack!" he called, and I leaped in beside the centerboard trunk just as the sail filled on the offshore side and pulled us away. He could handle a boat. I was full of excitement for Ruth and admiration for John. The sound of the water under us and the wind over us seemed just right.

It was a beat out of the harbor. We worked right up into the wind through the anchorage again and into the channel, then tight-tacked out the channel past Ram Island. You could see why it was called Ram Island, and why almost every little port town has a Ram Island: it was full of rams, boated out there to fight among themselves and to separate them from the gentler ewes. They were brought back only at breeding time.

Past the island and out of the channel we fell off on a long starboard tack that would take us halfway up the shore of Butler's Point, which pointed like a finger to Bird Island and its lighthouse a quarter mile offshore. We were passing across Ram Island's seaward shore when I said, "We're a little close to that big rock out here, aren't we?" I had dinged a propeller on it one day.

"Close, but it's further out. You can run inside it if you're — hold on, now." He sat up straight. "How did you know about that rock? As a matter of fact, Jack, there are a lot of things you know about, like where Hale Brook is and the road to Boston and the names of towns around here. And there are plenty of things you don't know about, like Teddy Roosevelt being President and what wars we've fought and such like. How would you like to explain that?"

"You sound angry."

"I'm not so angry as I am damn suspicious."

"You sound angry all the same."

"No such a thing."

"It sounds like you're angry that I paid some attention to Ruth."

"Dammit, Jack —"

"No, it sounds like you're good and mad that I made eyes at your girl."

"She's not my girl."

"You're luffing." He had let the boat too far up into the wind. It was a rare lapse in a natural waterman like John.

"I don't know whose girl she is."

"But not mine."

"I don't know! I don't know how I feel . . . how she . . . dammit, Jack. Why did you go and do that?"

"Do what?"

"Put your finger right on what's needling me. It's not the gentlemanly thing to do."

"Why not?"

"Because a fellow's got a right to his privacy." He showed a weak little grin and I knew, no matter what, we would always be friends. "You seem to know just what I'm thinking."

"Sometimes I do. That's because I know you better than you think I do."

"You must."

"I do. But I'm really sorry if I hurt you about Ruth."

"You didn't hurt me so much as confuse me. I've never really thought about Ruth as, well, as a girl. If you can catch my drift. I've just never, as it were, *thought* about it and, though she and I are excellent friends, I shouldn't . . . intrude on her private life. If you . . . see . . ." He was examining some little string in the main sheet with grave interest and was about to let *Captain Gnat* luff up again, but caught it just in time. John, and a lot of people I met then, had strong emotions but didn't look at them too closely. They felt a lot but didn't know what they felt.

"John, I'd like to tell you that I didn't think Ruth was much on looks and that she seemed sort of dull and prissy, but —"

He looked out across Buzzards Bay. "Then we'd both be perfect fools," he said. He reached under the seat and brought out the fishing box. He handed me a handline and a feathered jig. "Here. Try the Carter No-Fail Bucktail. I don't know anything about women but I can catch those fish. You do what you can and I'll do what I can and, between us, we'll do fine." You could do worse than have a friend like John Swain Carter.

We let out the lines and ploughed on. The wind was still up but not heavy. We didn't speak for a long time. Coming up on the Butler Point Shore we short-tacked out to gain seaway for the last leg to Bird Island. We fluttered around, the sail filled on the starboard side, the fishing lines made a graceful curve behind us, and John said, "You haven't answered my questions, though. And you haven't told me the secret you mentioned on number fifty-four. Do they go together?"

I watched the lines behind us. "Time to check them for weed?" I asked.

"Sure. Bring the lines in. Do they? Go together?"

I hauled in the lines, trying to drop them in coils the way Corbin Starkweather had. It worked pretty well. There were weeds on the lures. "Yes," I said, and I let the lures stream back behind us. "Yes."

He sat with the tiller under his arm. I wanted to tell him, and I was afraid to tell him. He waited.

"The thing I've got to tell you is going to be tough to believe. But I swear it's true though there's no way I can prove it to you."

"Jack, I —"

"Let me get through it, and then tell me how you feel about it.

"I could have come up from New York, but I didn't, or Maine or California or France or Russia, but I didn't. I came from Marion."

"Marion? Why, I know everyone in —"

"Let me finish the whole thing. It's tough enough. I didn't come from the Marion you know. I didn't come from another *place* . . ." I looked at the water streaming past, then back to John. "I came from another *time*."

He didn't understand yet.

"John, I was born in 1966."

The furrow between his eyebrows deepened.

"I was born in Tobey Hospital, in Wareham, in 1966. I figured it out: that's sixty-two years from now. I found a place, accidentally, and got caught in . . . something . . . in a time storm, and got thrown back to this time, your time. Look at me. Am I trying to trick you? Look hard."

"No."

"You know me. Am I crazy?"

"I don't think you are." He shook his head like someone who has just been hit.

"There's more. You may as well get it all at once. This thing happened on Penikese Island. In my day it wasn't a leper colony. When I was trying to get off the island, One-armed Higgins saw me and threatened me."

"That's why —"

"That's right. If he sees me he will raise a hell of a stink and people will start wondering where I *did* come from and I can't prove a thing."

"What else?" he said, shaking his head.

"Look at me. I'm your friend and I'm not joking with you and I'm *not* crazy, but if I didn't tell this to someone I'd go crazy. I'm telling you the truth because I have to, and you've got to believe me. You're my only chance. I got off Penikese, swam off in the middle of the night to Nashawena, then to Cuttyhunk, and then I got a ride to Marion because it's the only place I could think of to go."

"Did you . . . live in Marion?"

"My name is not Jack Stone."

"No, I guess not."

"My name is Jack Carter. I'm named after you. Goosefish Cove was the only place I could come to. I'm your grandson."

The boat luffed up into the wind and hung there with the sails slatting and banging above us, making a terrific racket, and we sat in the boat looking at one another, clinging to the gunwales as the little skiff was thrown about by the bay chop.

A wave broke beside us and the breeze caught the

spray and dashed us both in cold water. We looked around and found we were right across the outer harbor in the midst of Seal Rocks. We both leaped for the main sheet and backed the sail and picked our way out, barely missing some of the rocks, bumping our centerboard once or twice. In the clear again, we fell off for an easy reach to Bird Island and began to untangle the handlines.

John was shaking his head. "Jesus, Joseph, and Mary," he muttered. He looked confused and even dismayed. I moved aft, hesitating, then put my hand on his shoulder. He jumped, startled, and then looked at my hand as if it were burning him, but I kept it there. I knew then he believed me. He just stared at it for a moment with an expression of bewilderment. Then he reached up and put his hand on mine and looked me in the eye. "What now, Jack?" he said.

Like I said, you could do worse than have a friend like John Carter.

## CHAPTER TWELVE

# Bird Island

THE GUT between Bird Island and Butler Point is sheltered by bars but shallow. It was a long stretch of thin water to the beach and after our centerboard bumped the first time we pulled it up. We got the sail in, too, and brailed it up with its own mainsheet along the mast and sprit, then stowed the whole long parcel along the port side. Both sets of oars got stowed under the seats and both of us slid out of *Captain Gnat* into about two feet of water. We began to walk the boat in, one on each side, with the lap of the water around us and the wind over us and the wiry cries of the terns all around us. But we were quiet.

I was beginning to wonder if I had shared the load of my secret or just spread it around.

"Jack?" John said, and we stopped, holding the boat lightly, letting it nod between us.

"Yes?"

"I don't want you to go."

"Where?"

"Back."

"Oh, back. No. I don't think I want to go, either, but . . . I think I've got to."

"Why?"

"I don't know."

He nodded. He understood, I guess, as much as I did. We started toward the beach and I tried to explain: "It's my time there. It's my chance at living. My . . . turn, my turn at leading."

We walked in the shallows.

"This is your time and your turn to go into the future. I think you have to make your way and find out everything for yourself. I think I've got to do the same. If I don't, if I stay here — sometimes I want to very much — then I'm a robin trying to be a tern, or I'm trying to live someone else's life. It's confusing, but what feels right is that I *try* to get back and take my turn. Does that make sense?"

He nodded, but he did not look at me as we walked *Captain Gnat* in until it grounded flat out. He brought out the little one-armed anchor and I took Minnie's basket. He set the anchor at the length of its line and announced, "Tide's rising," and we waded for the beach. When we were on dry sand he stopped. He stared at the sand. "I'm afraid," he said.

"Sure," I said. "Me, too." I shifted the basket and put my free arm around him and we walked up the little rise to the lighthouse. "All I can tell you is that you're there."

"Am I?"

"Sure. I left the morning of your birthday. Sorry."

He giggled. "It's all right. Don't worry about it."

I giggled with him. It all sounded so damn foolish. "You're a nasty old fart."

"Am I?"

"No. I probably shouldn't tell you any more. But, you know, there's really not much I could tell you. I've never really known anything about my family, I never asked. Stupid."

"Will I — ?" He stopped talking. I knew what he was thinking.

"Right," I said. "We'd better have a rule. We don't know how this time business works. If I say the wrong thing to you it could be that we change the future. If we sneeze now maybe it causes a hurricane in the future, or maybe —"

"Or maybe you just disappear, snap, like Blackstone."

"Who?"

"Nothing." He grinned.

"Okay, the rule is this: no talking about the future, no revealing anything to happen. Agreed?"

"I think that's best."

"And let's try not to fret over it. We're both scared, but it's a kind of adventure."

We looked at each other and burst into laughter. A couple of ninnies! We would have plenty of worried times and plenty of late-night talk about it.

Mr. George Pickett leaned out over the railing around the lens house of the light, forty feet above us. "Missed 'em," he called down, pointing with a long telescope. "Went right through 'em, too." He drew back and we couldn't see him but soon began to hear him padding down the stone steps inside. The door banged as if hit with a hammer and swung out heavily, Mr. Pickett pushing with both hands. He walked directly past us without a glance and came to a stop at the edge of the grassy circle all around the lighthouse, where he unbuttoned his fly and relieved himself on the sand beyond. "No," he said, buttoning up his fly. "No, can't see a thing from down here. Nope." He turned back toward us and walked right past again, straight into the lighthouse, and we heard his steps start up. They stopped, waited, came back down, and he appeared in the light again, motioning impatiently for us to come along. He was almost a third of the way up when he climbed the first step. He climbed spryly for a man of, I guessed, sixty-five years, and we hurried after him on the narrow stairs that were part of the wall, a narrow spiral that wound around and up into the dark like a shaving from a thin-edged plank, like time.

A door opened at the top of the stairs and light reached down to us. When we reached it we found Mr. Pickett setting plates on a small table. There was also a small stove in the round room, a narrow bunk, two chests which Mr. Pickett was sliding to the table, and a comfortably padded chair beside a small bookcase. It was most like a ship's cabin, tidy and small, except for the roundness and the dazzling light, which came from two windows with broad, slanting sills and jambs, and from the hatch above into the lens house.

He set out a block of cheese and a knife, hard ship's crackers, and poured goat's milk from a saucer-topped pitcher into stoneware mugs. Goat's milk is rich and mellow, if you like it, musty and strong if you don't. Mine tasted a bit musty but I drank it. "Tea?" he asked, then answered himself immediately, "No. No, you'll be catching the last of the breeze, if that." He sat down on his bunk and put Minnie's basket in his lap. While we ate cheese and crackers, he clucked and murmured to himself with obvious pleasure as he laid the contents out on the bunk in a rigid pattern: two books from the Taber Free Library here, two jars of peach conserve here, one jar of lye pickles just here, a loaf of bread beside — no, over here, and (great delight with much clucking) four long cigars of the kind called stogies, which were laid carefully out in a fan shape. Also a paper packet of loose tea which made him look up and shrug. No time, last of the breeze.

He shot up suddenly and put everything away. Books, jars, bread, stogies, and tea. He put away the cheese and crackers from under our noses and took away our plates, tossing the crumbs out the window. He stood beside us until we got up, and with a scraping of chests and a quick brush of the table followed by a jerk of crumbs out the window, the room was the same as when we entered. He picked two pieces of horehound candy from a bowl and pushed them into our shirt pockets as if he were installing a wall hook. Then he plucked his telescope down from the wall hook and started up an iron ladder to the lens house. "Lively now," he said, still climbing, "before you go."

We scuttled after him as lively as we could and we were standing with him on the walk outside the house where we'd first seen him. He gave us his report.

"Blue, blue, striper, blue," he said, pointing with his telescope to one stretch of water, then another. "Squiteague, fluke, fluke, striper there but they only been catching 'em at evenin'." We followed him around the walk as he reported and pointed. "Bigelow boys been draggin' 'em in off the Bow Bells, drailing. Ike Thetford and Winifred Pojack have worked them cove waters, spoonin' more than fishin'. Clammin' no good along the whole East Shore of Butler Point. Quayhoggin' fair, bullraking, Wareham way." Then, pointing to Butler Point: "Someone ailin' at Whitesides, that or company, more sheets hanging out. Someone's shoat killed on Round Hill four days back, prob'ly: buzzards. Fishin's down from last year." We were back at our starting place on the walk. "You'll go back this way: in along the shore to the rock spill, drailin' with a bucktail, then harden up over toward the Fish Club, watchin' for weed. Then in the west edge of the channel till Ram Island's abreast. If you don't get into 'em by then, go home."

He was already down the ladder and starting down the stairs. When we got to the bottom he was waiting at the door with Minnie's basket. He handed it to us. "Mrs. Carter," he addressed us, holding up one finger for attention, "thank you."

"We'll tell her, Mr. Pickett."

He smiled and closed the big door in our faces, the iron latch hammered home, and we heard his footsteps pattering up the stairs. Live in a lighthouse and become a loony. Or was it that loonies picked lighthouses?

The West Shore of Butler's Point wasn't seeing any action. We brought in the sheet and headed across the outer harbor.

"How are you going to get back?" John asked.

"I don't know. At least I don't know exactly. I think I found a place where . . . sort of . . ."

He shook his head. "It's hard to think about it. There's no model, like a boat's half model."

"Maybe not, but here . . ." I handed him a plane shaving out of my pocket. "What if the world goes round and round, like the cutter of a wood bit, but it goes forward, too, just like a bit but into the future in a direction — or a dimension — we can't see: time."

"And?"

"It would make a spiral, wouldn't it?"

He pulled the curl out into a spiral while I held the tiller. "So?"

"Now, what if some days of the year are like the same days of every other year."

"What do you mean?"

"Like muggy summer days with the same sou'-wester and the same haze and the same bright glare and the same heat."

"Yes?"

"Bend the spiral. See how they touch? A year apart they touch, maybe on the same day, and if the spiral were long, if it went forever and bent back and forth, the years might touch. Like the Gulf Stream. You know about the Gulf Stream?"

"Certainly do. It swings in two days off Nantucket. What about her?"

"Well, I've seen satellite pictures of the Gulf Stream —"

"You mean like stereopticon views?"

"No, from high up."

"How do you get high up?"

"Never mind."

"Whoops. No questions."

"Right. Anyway it's not stable, not like a river in its banks. It curves around and meanders and changes shape like a snake, very slowly. It even curls back on itself and cuts into its own flow, and when it does that it spins off an eddy that wheels out into the ocean alone."

"Okay."

"So time could — might — curl back on itself and touch on one of those same days, one of the days that's the same every year. You see?"

"I think so, but how would you jump from one to the other?"

"Maybe in a place where the ice is thin."

"What?"

"When you go ice skating, there are always places you can't skate. The ice is too thin."

"Right. Springs come up under it and the earth-heat in the water melts the ice."

"Right. I'm thinking there might be places like that in time and space both, places where the flow of something keeps the surface between times thin."

We sailed on and he nodded. "Lord, though, we've got a problem."

"Right on," I said.

"What?"

"I mean, we sure as hell do."

"What can we do? How can we know anything about this? What if we find a thin place and fall right through? What if you go back — or forward — too far and, Lord's sake, *meet* yourself."

"Oh hell."

"Right on," he said.

"Whatever we do, it's got to be quick. I have the awful feeling I could be stranded and never get back. I wish we could talk to someone. I've gone just about as far as I can go with this thing."

"I'm afraid I can't help much with philosophical turns like this, Jack. I'm just a shop hand."

"You help more than you know."

"There is a fellow."

"Who?"

"Skiffs One and Two. The fellow who's having them built is Leander Allen Plummer. He lives in New Bedford and has a big summer place on Potomska Point. He's an engineer and a painter and a sculptor, but mostly he fishes and fools around with boats. He's a queer fellow, but deep."

"Can we talk to him?"

"Just about as nice a fellow as they come. Talk your leg off."

"When can we see him?" I asked.

"This week. We've got to go to New Bedford to get the rigs for One and Two. He's having them made up at the C. E. Beckman Loft. The two boats have twin hulls to test one rig against the other."

"We've got to see him. Someone has to help us to —" But the lines snapped then, and we were into the blues.

## CHAPTER THIRTEEN

# New Bedford

IT WAS early when we rowed to the Saltonstalls'
dock and picked up Ruth in the gentle first
light of the morning. She was not in a white dress
but in bib denims like ours, as shocking as it was for
the town and the time. She was barefoot and carried
a wide straw hat. As we drifted into the dock she
knelt to catch our rail. You know how it is that
early: quiet. You don't want to frighten the day before it's strong, so you speak gently, if at all. Colors
are quiet in that light. Shapes are plain.

The dory touched the dock with a soft, hollow

note. Ruth moved it along hand over hand, stepped lightly into the stern, and pushed off with her other foot, balancing there for a moment with her hands on the gunwales and her leg swung back like a dancer.

She was there the next morning, and the next. We drifted while Ruth slipped the rudder into its gudgeons, then we pulled away with the oars and she steered. We faced aft, she looked forward. Sometimes our eyes would meet and she would smile. Bending and leaning to the stroke of the oars I was close to her. We all caught fish and talked and laughed. When we came back into the harbor it was still early and the work went better through the day because we'd all been together.

Thursday it was raining. At eight in the morning we were standing by the tramcar tracks on Route Six, or what would be Route Six when it was no longer a wide, slippery mudway. It was slick and deep and difficult to walk across. The tram arrived clicking and rattling. It stopped with a squeal of sycamore brakes and a crackling flash from the electric line above, and we boarded.

Once I accustomed myself to the snaps from the pickup shoe above, and to the faintly yellow smell of the big electric motor under the floor, it was a pleasant ride. The roadbed was easy, and twice we passed gangs of gandy dancers: roadbed maintenance crews, who straightened and leveled the tracks by eye with a shuffling, lifting motion all together that gave them their dancer name.

We passed the Marion dude stop, where rich folks from Converse Point boarded, and rattled through pastures with occasional patches of woods to the Mattapoisett stop. We crossed the Mattapoisett River at the head of the harbor where freight wagons waited outside a mill. Oaks stood wide and hazy in the rainy fields. Then we crossed a swampy lowland bearded with maple and cedar, and into Fairhaven, which was lovely: small, all the streets green-arched with fine trees. There was a cathedral looking damp and delicate in the rain, and many good houses shingled and freshly painted: a neat little town that stopped as we broke out onto the Acushnet River bridge.

There are good things and bad things to say about that time. One thing is this: it looked better. The drive from Marion to the Acushnet River on Route Six today is ugly, confusing, even brutal, compared to the rides I took on that tram. A bare field with two pasture oaks doesn't ask anything. In the rain or under snow or baking in the sun it is balanced, at rest. The shopping malls along Six are full of chrome and light but not dignity like the oaks. A shopping mall is always out of balance.

Steam launches stitched ragged seams of smoke

across the Acushnet, lines that blew flat and faded themselves away. Masts, hundreds of them, pinned the low gray sky in place. New Bedford was low and gray, too, with only an occasional spire to emphasize the soft contour.

Nothing could have prepared me for the smell of New Bedford in the rain. It was a deep organic vapor, a presence more than a scent, that was released by the rain and rose up to capture the air. Mostly it was the horse manure, dried, beaten, and ground into fine powder by hooves and wheels, pressed into the chinks between a million granite and elm paving rocks, whirled up into drifts and wind devils on gusty days to powder felt hats and dark clothing with a delicate beige dust, dissolved on rainy days into a thin paste that clung to men's boots, shoes, and spats, and rimmed women's long skirts with a crusted hem. The body of the stench was manure but it had strong undertones of wet wool, horsehair, leather, privies, rancid whale oil from the docks, tar, burning coal and charcoal. It was overwhelming but not disgusting, neither pleasant nor unpleasant, just strong.

We walked up the hill past shop windows and many signs, small and large, lettered in a hundred fancy styles advertising dentists and osteopaths and hatters. In the vestibule of one store, wheeled in out of the rain, was a stuffed bear. We paused in front of the Wright Drug Company in the Cummings Building: *"Cool Soda . . . Fine Cigars . . . Fine Chemicals . . . Mineral Waters . . . Brushes . . . Fancy Goods . . . Surgical Instruments."* I looked through the window and John stopped beside me. There were ornate cabinets wth curved glass fronts, high shelves with ladders on tracks, and in the middle a tall wire pyramid filled with natural sponges. I stepped back from the window and instead of the store's interior I saw our reflection in the rain. In our borrowed foul-weather jackets, under our rubberized rain hats, we looked identical.

"Are you keen on a treat?" he shouted, as an unloaded freight wagon was passing. Eight iron-shod hooves and four steel-tired wheels crashed against the stone street and reverberated from the sounding board of the empty bed.

"Sure!" I shouted back. The teamster was reining in the horses and applying the squealing wooden brakes as the dray picked up speed down Union Street. With four wagons ahead of him and two laboring up the hill and a Union Railway horsecar clipping across the street above, the noise was deafening.

The New Bedford City Hall was a handsome building. It was new, gleaming white, and it had a guard of dense elms all around it with telegraph wires fastened directly to them. A town well stood in front with an octagonal teepee over it, an iron horse trough was set at one front corner, and a letterbox set in a stone post was at the other. Directly across the street from the Hall's steps was an ice-cream parlor. I suppose it was some mark of ice cream's popularity that the prize piece of real estate in the city was given over to an elegant temple devoted to its enjoyment.

Though our entrance did not cause stares, we were dressed in a shabby way compared to the other customers. The shop was all white: table tops, walls, and floors. A white-uniformed attendant was mopping up the dim tracks of customers as they came in out of the rain. It may be my imagination, but I'm sure he wiped especially hard behind us. Once inside, the smell was different: the almost too-rich smell of warm milk, the scent of vanilla and oranges and flowers and, strangely, a smell you couldn't quite put your finger on in a place like this: the smell of . . . "Fish!" I whispered to John.

He looked around him, to see why I was whispering, I guess. "What about fish?" he whispered back, unnerved.

"This place smells like *fish*," I said.

He looked at me for a long moment. "Of course," he said in a normal voice.

It was my turn to look around. "Why of course?" I whispered.

"What do you need for both fish and ice cream?" he asked me. I shrugged; this was his time, not mine.

"Ice. This place shares an icehouse with the fish-market in the other end of the building."

Of course. We sat at a wire, marble-topped table and had the specialty of the house, orange water ice. Once you got used to the smell of the place — of the orange and the old haddock — it was exotic and delightful.

Hawthorne Street was up over the crest of the hill. The streets were quiet, the grass lawns very green, the houses neat and prim. We turned into a gate with a carved wood plaque that read PLUMMER. We were still shaking rain from our hats when the door was opened by a young woman in a light gray dress with a white apron and a maid's white cap. She looked like she wanted to run out the door more than let us in. The reason for her discomfort came marching around the corner.

"Mary Ellen, the kitchen floor is *still* not in the condition I wish it to be."

"Ma'am!" The frightened maid's curtsy dipped like a fishing bobber and she scuttled off with her hands at her sides. The source of all this discomfort stood before us. Mrs. Plummer was hardly more than five feet tall with a face that just missed being pretty; it was a child's face, beautifully shaped and set with small, fine features, but the eyes — great, dark, violet eyes — belonged to a very large person who was worried and angry at the same time.

"Good afternoon, Mrs. Plummer, we —"

"Out," she chirped. "Out, out, out. You are *staining* my oriental. Out, around to the *rear* entrance." She was shooing us off her rug and back out onto the porch with flutters of her tiny hands, not looking at us but at our wet shoes. Have you ever had one of those little Chinese lapdogs yipping at you?

There was a tumbling on the stairs above. It was either a cardboard carton of books being thrown down, or one of those haphazard stair runners who never do get the hang of it but avoid breaking their necks because they're quick and agile enough. It was the latter, and he managed a stop on the landing with some difficulty. He had made his crazy descent holding a clockwork mechanism of some kind in one hand and a set of tiny screwdrivers in the other, but that's the way Leander Allen Plummer was: all lop-sided flurry on the outside and oiled logic at the center. As he stood grinning at us, several wood chips drifted down from his short work apron. Mrs. Plummer saw it, too. She emitted a muffled little squeal. I was on his side immediately.

"Oh my, I'm sorry, Mother," he said to his wife. "John, my boy, I'm delighted to see you. Come on, boys, come up to the playroom and —" He leaned over the bannister and more wood chips snowed down the stairs and into the hall below. "Genevieve!" he called, and then, "No, it's not Genevieve any more, is it? No, don't tell me . . . ah . . . Mary Ellen! Yes, that's it." He grinned at us again. "Mary Ellen! Some tea and cookies in the playroom! Come on, boys, I'm excited about the boats. The rigs are done. I want to tell you how they work so you can match them when you sail them down to Potomska." We excused ourselves past Mrs. Plummer, whose pale face was achieving some red around the cheeks and nose, and with several Excuse me's and Ma'am's, we went up behind Allen Plummer.

"Poppa! Poppa!" Two little girls in sailor suits came rumbling along the second-floor hall in a way that suggested they were very much his girls. "Brother is trying to take the fish out of the bathtub!"

"Perdition!" shouted Mr. Plummer. "Allen! Allen! What are you doing! I *need* that big fellow!" I sensed they were a great family for shouting down halls.

A boy of about eighteen appeared out of a doorway, wearing a robe and carrying a bluefish, which was struggling weakly. "I was about to take a bath, Father, when this" — he held it out, dripping — "*snapped* at me."

"You don't need a bath, Allen," he said, continuing his noisy climb up the stairs. "You look perfectly clean to me. Good boy!"

We followed him. There was a groan from the boy and delighted giggles from the girls, and we reached the playroom.

Allen Plummer's workshop and study and office occupied the entire third floor of his large house. I knew at once that Mrs. Plummer never came here. The walls were covered with books, and glass cases of collections, and stuffed heads of deer and moose and antelope and even a lion peering out at you. You could be locked in that room for a month and, if someone sent in sandwiches, never be bored. There were broad oak tables with long tool racks down the centers, neat boxes of parts beside half-completed ship models and small machines. There was a high drafting table near one of the windows, and over it hung T squares and triangles and curves. There was a rolltop business desk with papers in baskets, and on the wall beside it, a blue porcelain button-plate marked *Western Union*. There were a treadle lathe and a painter's easel and racks of rifles and fishing rods. That room had everything. Dominating one end was a large rectangle, like a huge painter's canvas, but wooden, with the light from the end windows behind it.

"It's the leading edge, you see." He was talking to John and me about the rigs we were to pick up. "That's what does the work. Here, you can see it in the cross section, a wing, for that's all a sail is, a vertical cloth wing." Plummer brought down what looked like a Canada goose's wing from a shelf. "The gaff sails most boats use are adapted from the square sail: they're attempts to present a maximum area of resistance *downwind*. But yachts don't sail in the trades, generally, and so they sail *upwind* as much as *downwind*."

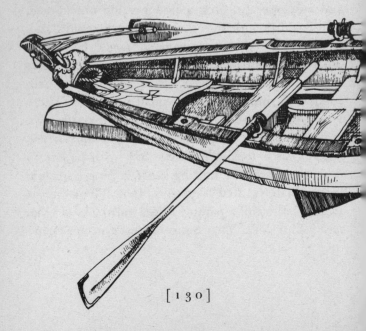

"The gaff sail is, certainly, a great advance and follows nature, in a way." He brought down a gull wing then and held it vertically, working the stiffened joint up and down a little, and it was very like a gaff sail. "But its leading edge is cluttered with hoops and brails and lines. No, it must be clean for the wind to slide across it without *wrinkling* itself. Now, here is the new hardware Herreshoff has sent over, you see?" He showed us a two-foot section of mast with a metal track screwed to it and metal runners that slid along it, the same kind of hardware you see on every boat today. "Clean, uncluttered . . . ah, thank you, Mary Ellen."

The maid was almost a different person in this room. She smiled and set out the silver tea things and cups and saucers and a plate of cookies. With our foul-weather coats off and our damp cuffs beginning to dry, the hot tea tasted good. It was a dark, strong tea with a delicious taste that I've never had again. Mary Ellen disappeared and John and Mr. Plummer were at the drawing board looking over line drawings of the skiff's riggings, talking about centers of effort and resistance and other things I didn't understand. I wandered along the tables and bookshelves to the far end of the room and came around to the window side of the large wood rectangle.

Leander Allen Plummer may have been an engineer and a painter, but he was also a master carver, and I was looking at his masterwork.

Art can capture time, can hold a moment of it frozen for you to see. This was the Bay, a moment of violence and beauty and power cut into the wood. He knew the Bay, it had to be that way. The curving bodies of bluefish sliced through a school of sand dabs. The blunt heads, the vicious mouths, the frightened confusion of the dabs, the waves, the waves, and above everything the terns darting, swooping, diving, all held, all still, a razor slice of time held in wood.

I looked down the room to Plummer. He was gesturing with a pen at the goose wing, excited, laughing as he spoke. He did not seem to match the carving. He was too light, too young, too open. But again I could see that he was one person outside, and inside, a colder, older man. Maybe all artists have that otherness in them. He was a good man to ask about time.

"I'm sure you will see the masthead rig with fittings very like these in all future yachts," he was saying. He was sure of himself, the engineer-artist.

"Is this the future, then?" I asked across the room.

"For yachting, yes, and Herreshoff himself is the future."

"I'm sorry to interrupt, sir, but the future is a subject that fascinates me."

"Good, good, don't apologize, my boy. The future is where we all shall live. For any thinking person, the fascination with times and ways to come never flags. I, too, find the years to come preoccupying. But do forgive me. I have been so preoccupied, my enthusiasm has gone ahead of my courtesy. I am Allen Plummer." He extended a tanned, firm hand.

"Jack Stone, sir. I'm a new apprentice at the Carter yard."

He looked carefully at me, cocked his head to one side and the other, then looked back at John. "You are cousins," he said.

"No, sir," I said.

"Ah, but you must be. You could easily be brothers. The resemblance is there. You must see it."

"Only friends, sir."

"Well, extraordinary, but then friends may come to look like one another, perhaps?" Perhaps.

"The future, sir."

"Time and the future, yes. Sit down there, Jack, and tell me about it."

"Sir, I want you — I would greatly appreciate *your* views on time; its structure, how it works."

He looked at me shrewdly for a moment, a long moment. He shook his head slowly. He looked like an engineer now, calculating forces. "I have a feeling," he said, "that you have been thinking seriously about the very things you ask me to speak of. Tell me, Jack, what you think of time. I may be able to pick up a thread and follow it."

"Yes, sir. I have been thinking of time. I have been thinking of time's shape." And I told him all I could: too little.

As he listened, he seemed almost asleep, hands folded, head down, though I could see his eyes blinking. He seemed deeply interested, and once he looked up with extra attention as I was describing the Gulf Stream's eddies. Then I was done. He did not move for a minute or more. He rose and walked to his desk and pressed the button in the Western Union wall plate.

The tea in our cups was cold. The rain outside continued.

He filled our cups and sat down once more. He picked up the clockwork mechanism he had been working on when we arrived and he held it before him. "I have thought about time. For me, for anyone, there is never enough time." He gestured with the collection of gears and sprockets at the crowded room full of projects. "And I have always wished to expand my limited supply. But it is not as simple as this little instrument. Look at it. It ticks, its gears crawl about, its hands spin at some given rate. Too simple. Too stable.

"Time is not measured out in ticks. Only man's

machines measure things so. Time is part of nature and answers to a higher motion. Time is tuned to the rhythm of the stars."

A noise on the stairs. Mary Ellen appeared, followed by a boy in uniform a few years younger than John and me. "Mr. Plummer," she began.

"Yes, Mary Ellen, it's quite all right." Plummer stood at his drafting board, writing swiftly. "Here. And this is for extra speed." He gave him the paper and a coin, and the Western Union boy was gone.

Plummer picked a flexible metal tube from the wall and blew into it. It made a little squeal back at him and he put the speaking tube to his mouth. "Sean, hitch up Hector and Lysander to the phaeton. We'll be taking them out as soon as you have the rig ready." A tiny voice spoke back and Plummer continued, "No, you stay dry, Sean, we don't need you this afternoon."

"Boys, fill up your pockets with those cookies. The girls will only eat them. We have a visit to make. You have asked me for my opinion and my best advice is to bring in a consultant who has made this field his own. And besides that" — he paused in putting on his own raincoat — "I believe you may add something to his knowledge."

"Just a moment, sir." I turned back to look at the huge carving again.

"Ah, you enjoy my little hobby?"

"More than a hobby, sir. You have caught and held time, here, if only a moment."

"A sham, merely an artifice. But enough of this. Our consultant awaits us. Come. You can see it again in a day or so." And we went down the stairs.

But he was wrong. I was not to see Allen Plummer's carving of the bay again for seventy-seven years.*

---

* You can see Leander Allen Plummer's carving today, hanging in the New Bedford Public Library, which was the Town Hall.

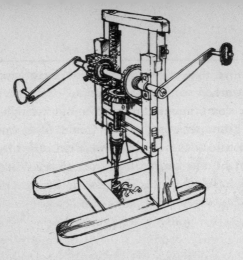

## CHAPTER FOURTEEN

# *The Oxbow*

THE CARRIAGE had isinglass windows stitched into coated canvas side flaps, but there was no windshield. We wore our slickers and covered our laps, as we sat across the single seat, with a canvas throw. When the wind brought rain from the side or rear we were sheltered, and when it was ahead of us it was no worse than walking in it. The horses' tails were braided and done up with little buckled straps. I think it kept them out of the muck thrown up at the shield in front of our feet (I remember Plummer calling it the dashboard), which came with the clopping rhythm Hector and Lysander worked to. They seemed to enjoy their work. John complimented Mr. Plummer on the horses. Mr. Plummer was obviously proud of them and had a real affection for the pair. He held the reins and a stiff whip in gloved hands but never struck the horses; the whip was a gentle tool for a driver like him, a longer reach to keep physical touch with them. John and Mr. Plummer talked about horses and horsemen, politely at first, then keenly with opinions and favorites. Most of it was completely over my head but I could see that "horseflesh," as they put it, was a necessary passion in a time when automobiles were a toy and, after all, only machines. Hector and Lysander were *friends*.

We came down the hill and back across the Acushnet River. Plummer turned the horses along the shore and then up toward the cathedral we had seen from the tram. He reined them into a driveway and under a portico directly across the street from the church's wet, gray spire. He hitched the horses and loosened their harness, then began to strip the water from their backs and sides and legs with a curved blade while we unfolded two blankets for them. When they were warm and comfortable, he gave them each an apple from his slicker pocket and we walked up to the door.

"Allen Plummer and friends. I believe we are expected."

"Yes, Mr. Plummer. Mr. Lynch is out of town today but Mr. Clemens is expecting you." I believe this fellow was actually a butler. "May I take your coats, gentlemen?" Oh, it is a heady feeling to be lumped in with gentlemen by an actual butler.

The house was all woodwork, blond oak for the better part, with light fir floors, varnished, and white pine wainscoting. I was getting familiar with wood.

"Al Plummer! You're a corn plaster for the soul on a day like this."

I noticed dark walnut chairs, looking very elegant against the light floors and oriental rugs, in a group around the fireplace, where a small fire ticked and snapped, welcome more for the dryness than the heat on a rainy day. The man looked large and familiar.

"Sam, good to see you! You must meet the young men I telegraphed you about. This is Mr. John Swain Carter, and this curious thinker is Mr. Jack Stone. Boys, this is Mr. Samuel Langhorne Clemens."

My head snapped back from the fire, and it was him. A loose white suit, a top-heavy loft of white hair and mustache and eyebrows almost hiding a pair of devilish eyes and a rumpled grin. "You're Mark Twain," I blurted out.

"By God! You're right. Damn, I've been trying to remember who I was since lunchtime. Glory, that calls for a drink. Woolwind! Windworth! Worthwhile! Whatever your name is, bring us in a drink for my perspicacious friend!"

"Mr. Twain, I'm sorry, I —"

"Sam, just Sam to you boys. Now, here" — the actual butler brought in a tea tray with decanters and glasses and plates of biscuits — "can I offer you fellows some Kentucky drying agent and a cigar?"

"No, sir, thank you."

"Well. I won't force you but I will advise you." He poured glasses of bourbon for Plummer and himself. "Acclimate yourself to the vices gradually and sensibly. Start early and make a good job of it. Now, I began at eight and feel it was none too early, but it has taken me over sixty years to accustom myself to this liquid vice — and on some mornings I think of myself as a pure novice. As for tobacco, I came into this world asking for a light and intend to exit through a smoke ring." And with his bourbon glass in one hand, he blew a round, pungent smoke ring and settled back in his chair to admire it.

Plummer poured John and me what we found to be grape juice from another decanter and offered us the plate of biscuits, saying, "Sam, we had a talk I wanted you to be a part of. It's uncanny, in a way, how Jack here has followed discussions we have had. Discussions of time. He has followed patterns deeply and skillfully for one so young — excuse me, Jack — and there is a tone of anxiety I could not fail to note."

Sam Clemens looked at me. The humor in his face never faded, but I saw now that his eyes were more than puckish. They were sad eyes, searching. The great fits of white hair all around his head distracted your attention from those tragic eyes.

"Time is the iron master," he said, "the moving finger, the pendulum of destiny, and, at the end, the reaper's blade. Looking backward, time is clearer than the present but, looking forward, as black as a Mississippi River night, revealing nothing.

"And very like a river, flowing down in one direction, down to some future sea. But everything seems like a river to me, for I seem irretrievably drawn to the happiest and most useful part of my life on the river. Oh, how I have wished that I could traverse this . . . this River of Hours and Tears as I did the smaller but nobler Mississippi: above the elegant power of a steamboat. I wish that I could pilot a time boat that would glide downstream or push upstream or, with a judicious hand on the telegraph, stop in midstream and watch the flow. I think I would be a constant traveler.

"But there is no steamboat plying these waters, nor no berth for a pilot that I have heard of. So we drift without help for it, with no way to reach another landing on the bank."

"The bank," John said thoughtfully. "If you go ashore you could walk upstream or down. Or take a shortcut across land athwart a bend in the river."

"Oxbows," Clemens said. "The river will curl back on itself in flat country and eat away at the banks a foot or two a day, like a great serpent, brown and slow, shifting its coils." He peered through the golden bourbon at the fire. "Sometimes the coils work so close as to touch. There is a great sigh of land giving way, a commotion in the current, and within mintues the flow has cut through the narrow oxbow, made an island of the surrounded land, and bypassed the loop almost entirely. You've got to read the river and put it in your head tightly, remembering every feature, but lightly, so as to encourage the thousand erasures and revisions every trip will offer. For the river never rests. No. It changes without ceasing and, like time, continues ever on."

"I can see it as a river," I said, "or as a spiraling curl, or as a wood bit boring through space, or as many things. But I can't get closer to the idea of stepping from one place in time to another than your river oxbow. Is it possible, is it a commonplace event?"

"No, no. If it were, who would stay put? Who

would ride out the storms of his own generation, when calls from the romantic battles in the past and the wonders of the future beckon?"

"I think most of them would stay, if they knew . . . what I think . . . they would find out." I was too close to the dangerous truth. Plummer was looking at Clemens and the eyes beneath those great brows were fixed on me. There was a hush. I could hear the rain, the fire, and a snort from one of the horses outside. I had said too much.

The writer's gaze lapsed and once again he looked through his whiskey at the flames. He was framing a question. We waited.

"Jack," he said, "do you believe it is possible for a . . . a person to cross from one place in time to another without . . . traveling the time between?"

He knew. Or was it only that he wanted to know, wished a thing to be possible? Was the intensity in his gaze inquiry or pleading? He will not press for an explanation, I thought, because he is afraid of this not being true, but I knew we were working behind a delicate wall that separated our convenient fiction from truth, using it as a tool to talk without fear of the large and frightening movements on the other side. If that wall broke, there would be too many questions, too many loose ends, too many proofs. It was a wall we used in politeness and respect. I made my answer with equal care.

I looked him in the eye. "There is no doubt in my mind." Plummer began to speak, but Clemens cut him off by rising between us and pouring him another dollop of bourbon. With his back to me he said, "I wrote a book."

"Yes, sir," I said, "a great book, *A Connecticut Yankee in King Arthur's Court*. I am sure that it will be read and admired — in 1982."

John was worried, frowning. I shook my head at him very slightly: It's all right. Plummer was excited. "Sam," he began, but Clemens cut him off again and drawled, "Settle down now, Al. Take a sip of that and sit back in your chair, there."

"In your book you have the Yankee going, leaving his own time, by accident, and returning by accident. But you don't have him trying to return."

"No. Should he?"

"I think so. I think he would feel out of place, out of balance; no matter how good he was at acting or learning new things, he wouldn't fit. He would be drawn back to the life he left unfinished. He would try. He would look for a way back."

John looked at me again, no longer worried. Concern and understanding were in his face. Clemens picked up a biscuit and stepped to the hearth nibbling at it. "He would return by the same route that brought him. He would go the way he came;

anything else would be too great a chance, too great a risk. Could he do that?"

"The oxbows," I said, "are places as well as changes. They would be real locations in both worlds where reality or space or time was drawn too thin, as thin as to slip through, across the oxbow to the same *place* but a different *time*. But I see now that the times would have to be similar, too. One day like another."

"Equal to equal," Allen Plummer said, "from a day here to its mate there."

"Like the smoky sou'westers in August," John said.

"Yes." Plummer was seeing it all. "A backflow of time through this . . . thin spot, this portal. The year has its cycle, the days and seasons correspond in a precise rhythm. An August day's departure, an August day's return; September out, September back."

My heart sank. Would I wait a year until I had a chance of returning? For the first time I imagined my mother and father's sadness, their fears, their uncertainty. My friends, even my dippy sisters. They loved me. I had been so busy trying to find myself that I hadn't thought of them. To them I was lost, dead, run away, taken, murdered. What was it like for them? I would have bawled right there if Sam Clemens hadn't spoken.

"No," he said, and it had the pilot's ring of authority, the same note of command that was in Captain Carter's voice when he backed off One-armed Higgins. Clemens took out a fresh cigar and a bone-handled knife. "Too long. This is not a common event, or citizens would disappear wholesale. Step into thin spots and turn up kicking and squealing on a dinosaur's doorstep. No.

"Time is a river and it's restless in its banks. It will shift one way and another. It will make an oxbow but not permanently. Come next election day, that oxbow will be gone. Shifted out." He snipped the cigar end into the fire where it flared and was gone. His knife closed with a snap.

"Everyday that you wait, every day the traveler in time waits, decreases his chances of returning. He may find another route through his thin spot, to the future or the past. Or worse; he may find *half* a route. No." The smoke surrounded him again and he cast the spent match into the fire. "This year, now, as soon as possible. That is when the traveler should make his try for it. August out, September back, for the days will match up for a time, but we do not know how long."

The butler knocked gently and opened the door. "Will the gentlemen be staying for lunch, sir?"

"Allen?" Twain asked.

"Sam, I think we all have work to do. We'll take

our leave of you and I'll see you later. This evening, I believe?"

"If that's what been laid on for me, Allen, I will allow Wutherymple in there to trice me up in that funeral suit and appear like a Barnum attraction."

At the door he shook our hands. He reached into his pocket and brought out his bone-handled knife. "Jack" — he gave it to me — "in grateful remembrance of your assistance and your ideas. I have the feeling we may not see each other before you — before I leave." Those eyes were deep but still very young. It made me want to say something.

"I think people will read *Connecticut Yankee* and *Tom Sawyer* and your stories for a long time, but I'm sure that writers many years from now will say that *Huckleberry Finn* is one of the best books America ever produced. Mr. Twain, I —"

"Sam," he said, "plain Sam Clemens. Luck, Jack."

We didn't talk much on the way back to New Bedford. The rain continued. Allen Plummer was excited but cautious, still careful of the wall. We drove to C. E. Beckman's long granite building on Commercial Street and left with twine-wrapped bundles of sails, twine-gathered clutches of sail hoops, and a lumpy parcel of Captain Herreshoff's sail-track hardware. Mr. Plummer drove us to the tram station.

"Do you boys have everything?"

"Yes, sir."

"Very well. You'll sail the skiffs down, then, and, believe me, I will understand if it takes longer than you expected. Please use the skiffs to advantage. Try them out, boys. Jack, I wish you well. I wish you both well. I will see you, John, with news of anything interesting. From Marion way," he added.

I nodded to John. "Yes," John said, "you will hear the news and we will bring the skiffs."

"You are good, brave boys. In woodcarving you must work boldly, but with care. Go with the grain. I trust that lesson is not lost on you."

"No, Mr. Plummer. Thank you so much for everything," I said. The tram started and Mr. L. A. Plummer stayed behind, beside Hector and Lysander. His derby hat was slick and shining in the rain as he took it off to us. I could see him smiling, blinking in the rain, a gentleman.

Recrossing the Acushnet, John said, "I think we know what to do."

"Yes."

"Tomorrow. We can work tonight on the rigs and leave for Penikese tomorrow."

On the ride back to Marion we discussed our plan. We would try the gray rains of September as a pair of connecting days. We would sail together to

Penikese in the two skiffs and John would wait on Cuttyhunk through a tide. If tomorrow didn't work, another set of days, and another.

The New Bedford road was no less muddy when we got off at Marion. We walked along Front Street in the rain, carrying the dark red sails on our heads like heavy, tar-fragrant rain hats. We turned down Hiller Street just as Mrs. Crapo was coming out her door holding an earthenware casserole in a towel. Its hot sides steamed in the rain. As she saw us her face clouded.

"Oh, Johnny Carter," she said, "I'm so sorry."

John turned and started toward the boatworks as fast as the sail and the hardware let him. I caught up with my sail flouncing and the sail hoops clattering. His face was grim.

"What's the matter?" I shouted.

"Someone is sick, or dying, or dead," he said, and kept on running.

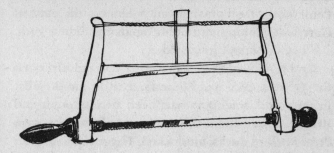

## CHAPTER FIFTEEN

# *Death*

THE SAILS hit the floor one after the other; the hoops and hardware followed. Skiff One and Skiff Two cruised regally up the centerline of the workshed, new-finished, freshly painted. The shop was swept and neat, things in their place. It was all in order, except for a tumble of tools at the end of the window counter. Someone had knocked over a box of gouges; they were strewn on the counter. Some lay on the floor beside a cracked whetstone, one skew chisel was stuck upright in the planking. A dark stain of oil was spread around a tin marked *Neatsfoot,* soaking into a blue bandanna.

"The Captain," John said.

In the kitchen there were other covered dishes on the table, a pie, some flowers, a little jar of jelly. Friends and neighbors had been here. Rough and strange beside these tidy offerings of concern were three mallard ducks, unplucked: Higgins.

I did not have much time to wonder why the relationship between the Captain and Higgins was so complex. There were footsteps on the stairs; Minnie was coming down. We went to her.

She had been crying, but was not crying now. We two boys just surrounded her and held her. "Oh, Mom," John said, and I said, "Minnie."

"The Captain," she began, paused to rest her forehead on John's shoulder, then continued. "He had a seizure in the mid-morning. I heard him fall. We got him up to bed and called Dr. White. We made him comfortable and Reverend Thomas came down. He passed on just before noon. He asked me who the officer on deck was, then he said, 'Minnie, open that curtain, will you?' and when I came back he was gone."

We had wanted to comfort Minnie when we both held her, to give back some of the love that came from her, but we were crying now, and once again,

it was Minnie who was comforting us. Comfort
came out of her like a spring from a mountain. The
three of us stood there together, and then she said,
"I'm going to need some help. With the Captain."

"Yes, Mom."

"Jack, there's no need for you to help."

"I'll help you, Minnie. I feel like —"

"We feel like you're family, too, Jack. Well, then,
let's get the Captain ready."

And we did. There was nothing scary or disgusting about it. There was no hearse full of somber
professional handlers to take him away. We were his
family, and we did what we could to prepare his
body to be seen by his friends. The body was lying
on his bed. Minnie took the sheet away and the only
shock was that it had no clothes. "The doctor helped
me with his work clothes," Minnie explained, fold-
ing the sheet. "Your father has gone to arrange the
church and the grave."

Minnie took the coins from the eyes and untied
the cloth that kept the jaw closed. She did this for us,
so we could see the face, and she left the room. If
there was any expression on the Captain's face it
was relief, like a runner closing his eyes after a long,
painful run. It was a look that had won over pain
and weariness.

Minnie came back with hot water and soap. John

and I washed the body all over, an old strong body with wrinkles, folds of skin. I was washing a shoulder and said, "Minnie?"

"That is a cutlass wound," she said simply.

There were other wounds, a missing toe. We washed and dried carefully. Already the joints were getting stiff. Minnie and the doctor had bound the Captain's hands together with cloth wraps, which we cast off to do our work. Minnie shaved his face with his own razor and brushed his hair and trimmed his mustache. John and I scrubbed the old, scarred hands while Minnie went to the attic. Cleaning the nails, we were careful not to hurt him, but of course if wasn't him any more. Minnie came back with a long, camphor-smelling package, and out of the thin packing she took the splendid full-dress uniform of a Union Navy captain, with gold braid and epaulets and a hat with a black egret feather. We put the uniform on him in silence, admiring his buttons, and Minnie pinned on a row of decorations.

"I don't know that there's a right order," she murmured, "but I do not think anyone will mind. After the funeral these medals are to be yours, John. And the sword. He made that clear a long time ago."

"Thank you, Mother."

"What? Oh, no. Thank — well, he knew you would feel thankful."

We were retying the chin bandage and binding

the hands when Joshua returned. He had been crying, too, but in his secret, private way. He stood in the doorway.

"I know we are full of grief at this time," he said, and his voice sounded very close to cracking, "but we must try not to show our feelings."

Minnie lowered her eyes and said, "Yes, Joshua."

Joshua strode to the bed and measured his father's body for a coffin. Who could build one better? But I saw the boxwood rule shaking as he took the dimensions.

Minnie placed the coins back on the eyes and we all left the room. We boys followed Joshua to the work shed, while Minnie began to prepare more food and a clean house for the Captain's friends.

"Cedar," Joshua said, "native cedar. In the drying shed." And he gave us a wave of the hand that sent us off to get it.

We worked all afternoon. We spoke now and again, not solemnly but quietly. We were all thinking of him. It was my job to bring down the cedar to thickness and finish, just as the Captain had taught me. I did a very good job. When John and I went in for a late lunch of tea and some cheese, Minnie was cleaning the parlor with Mrs. Crapo, smiling and chatting. Death came, but not as a dread stranger. Death and life, winter and summer, the cycle of the year and its precise rhythm: Minnie and John and

Mrs. Crapo were close to the turning stream of time.

Joshua, though, was all inward. So much like my own father. He showed no outward emotion. But when we returned after our snack, I watched him fitting the planks I had planed: small damp spots stained the light wood and I did not think they were sweat.

We worked into the evening. Joshua finished a plain, handsome coffin. Both of us wanted to be near him. As an excuse, we finished out the rigs of Skiffs One and Two. Minnie was baking one last batch of small cakes when we carried the coffin in; we all went up to the Captain's room and placed the body inside. Then, all together carried it down and set it on sawhorses in the parlor. Minnie went up to bed.

We had been through a long day. I did not think I could be so calm, so peaceful after such a time, but the death of the Captain had a dignity and a place in everything. It was handled with all proper sorrow but no shame or frustration. I felt close to life. John and I washed up behind the kitchen.

"Tomorrow," he said.

"The funeral?"

"After the funeral, then we go."

"But all the visitors, the cemetery . . ."

"In the morning. Minnie will think we want to get off alone, and she'll be right."

"I guess so. I'll want to."

"If what Mr. Clemens says is true, we've got to get you to Penikese as soon as we can."

"John, I don't want to leave you, or Minnie, or Joshua."

"I know. I know."

"I don't want to leave any of it. Ruth."

"I know, Jack. It's just the way things are. It's the way things have to go."

"Like the Captain."

"Like the Captain."

John went up first to say good night to Minnie. I toweled off and walked past the closed parlor door. Inside I could hear Joshua Carter talking low, talking on and on, making his peace with all the things he hadn't said, talking to the Captain. I left him to it and went up the stairs.

## CHAPTER SIXTEEN

---

# A Service

JOHN HAD a black church suit. I had only the overalls and a denim shirt, but they were clean. I do not think anyone took offense. For that matter there was not much difference between working clothes and formal clothes. After all, carpenters were building the new house on Cottage Street dressed in dark wool trousers, vests, shirts, ties, and derby hats, with sometimes a nail apron. Of course Corbin Starkweather arrived in his black suit and hat with his wife beside him.

"Mrs. Carter, I am so sorry for you at this hour of despair. Loretta and I are both at a loss to express our hearts' distress." Corbin's feet looked small and pointed in the patent-leather shoes he wore. I noticed, because he left his boots beside the door on the porch; he would probably be pulling pots after the service. The Bay wouldn't wait. His words sounded flowery and more like decoration than sense, but his voice was honestly sad, and he was trying to comfort Minnie with the depth of his concern. His wife was young and pale and pretty, but she had bad teeth. Corbin went to Joshua, who shook his hand without expression.

Corbin said, "He was a good man on the water and a shrewd businessman." That was all he said, as if those two notations were the highest parts of virtue and all other goodness naturally followed them. Then he came to me.

"Jack," he said, "I heard the Captain speak of you hopefully." From any other figure this mere expression of hope would be a small and faint recommendation but the Captain was a hard man, and that skeptical word of hope from him was worth a mouthful of praise from anyone else. It felt good.

"Thank you, Mr. Starkweather." He nodded briskly and moved on to John, but I could see he was near crying. He shook John's hand and clapped

him on the shoulder in a rough and doubtless painful way that showed he was a little out of control.
Then he went quickly from the room.

The damp handkerchief ladies, on the other side
of the room, were in a happy ecstasy of crying and
pity. They would flutter in from the latest long look
at the Captain's body and hug Minnie and lean
against Joshua (whose shoulders remained rigid and
whose eyes fixed and refixed on the wall opposite
him) and tell him the Captain was "in a Better Place
with his Maker," and that he looked "so peaceful,
just as if asleep." No way. He looked dead: pale as
milk, sunken eyes, and surrounded by flowers that
were more for their masking fragrance than decoration.

No, it wasn't horrible. It was real, though. I
watched the faces of several men as they looked
over the body. Their expressions were grimmer and
resigned. They were looking ahead to their own
times and death was not far away.

Maybe in a time when emotional expression was
so tight and proscribed, the damp handkerchief ladies needed a chance to let go. Maybe looking at the
body was a rite of finality, and comforting in a way.
The only thing that bothered me about it was that all
the words and snuffling were not like the Captain,
and I wanted them to be.

Standing there in the parlor, I began to think of

John Swain Carter's birthday party on the day I left. He would have liked the party and he would have liked the speech I was to give him. Stranger still, the thought of it made me want to giggle. I looked across to John and smiled.

The door was thrown open. It knocked a teacup out of a woman's hand. The cup shattered on the oak floor, and One-armed Higgins lurched into the parlor. He was drunk, and a vase of flowers went down as he leaned against the coffin, crying.

I do not know what tie of affection and anger — for it was certainly both — was between the Captain and Higgins. No one ever told me. Higgins stood over the body; suddenly he raised his hand as if to strike it — a general gasp from the ladies — and then he broke down entirely, and his raised fist came down as if pulled by his sobs. He checked himself for a moment, drew himself up, tears streaming over his unshaven cheeks, and saluted. That is the only clue I have. Joshua stepped forward and led him easily into the kitchen.

Had Higgins served under the Captain? Had he lost his arm on the Captain's ship? Did he hate him or love him or both? I do not know. I was to have no time to find out.

People were leaving quickly. Joshua nodded to the minister, who nodded to John. When John and I were alone in the room, we turned to our work.

Higgins had me scared. I was too close to making some sense out of this whole crazy situation. The trip back to Penikese: I dreaded, hated, feared the trip, but my mind was drawn toward it, the attraction of something that seemed inevitable, unavoidable. There was some kind of comfort in it. I could fail, I could disappear, I could be thrown forward or back or be . . . It was too much.

"Easy, Jack. Take it easy. You're shaking." The flowers I was moving were quivering and water was splashing out.

I reached across the Captain's body and took John's hand. The shaking slowed and my stomach untwisted. "Damn," I said, "and double damn."

We laid the sword and the medals on a table and lifted the coffin lid up and into place. The pilot holes had been drilled. We used boat clouts, thick nails cut at the Tremont Factory in Wareham and hot-dipped in zinc. We drove them in slow and careful. When we looked up from the last nail, Joshua stood in the doorway with two pallbearers: Higgins and Corbin Starkweather.

Higgins is too preoccupied, I told myself. He won't recognize me — maybe.

John and I were at the head, Joshua stood in the doorway. Corbin and Higgins looked across the foot at one another with a chilling, hateful stare that wasn't diminished by Higgins's bleary eyes twitching to focus. Corbin began, "Higgins, you —," and Joshua said, "Please." It was the first word I'd heard him speak that day.

We lifted the coffin and marched out behind Joshua into the gray light under a troubled sky.

"After the service," John said. We walked behind the wagon carrying the coffin. "The skiffs are ready. Food and blankets. I've told Minnie."

"And Joshua?"

He shook his head and we both looked ahead to Joshua's striding, solemn figure. His hands swung at his sides, his shoulders tight, his head rigidly forward. Starkweather walked with his wife farther on. Higgins slumped beside the driver on the wagon, drinking from a bottle until it was empty. When we crossed Spring Street, he threw it aside and it shattered beside the road.

Ruth was there. She rode one of her father's brown mares at a slow walk. Her dress was black. Her face above it was pale and very beautiful. It was beautiful like Minnie's face, not in bones or features but in its giving, in its concern. I will always love those two faces and the women who filled them.

It was raining now. A light sprinkle. It settled the dust, and the smell of wet grass and leaves came up. It may have been my imagination, but the first thin splinter of autumn seemed to be carried by the rain.

We slid back the coffin and lowered it onto a pair of manila lines. I found my eye inspecting all the boat clouts, snug and well set, and the joints, true and even, and the finish of the rain-wet cedar. Good enough. Better than that. We lifted the coffin by the lines slung under it and walked it over the deep cut of the grave, two on a side. We lowered it until the earth at the bottom took its weight. John dropped his end of the line and Corbin Starkweather, standing across from him, pulled it under and up, coiling it with his quick, neat strokes. I dropped mine and looked to Higgins as he began pulling it through. The line made a hollow rasping against the coffin. He looked at me hard. The rain was streaking his hair over his eyes and he stopped pulling at the rope, but he was still looking at me. The minister began.

"One generation passeth away, and another generation cometh: but the earth abideth for ever. The sun also ariseth, and the sun goeth down, and hasteth to his place where he arose."

He stared at me.

"The wind goeth toward the south, and turneth about unto the north; it whirleth about continually, and the wind returneth again according to his circuits."

One-armed Higgins said quietly, "You." He said it to me. "You killed him," but the minister and the rain continued.

"All the rivers run into the sea; yet the sea is not full; unto the place from whence the rivers come, thither they return again."

"You," said Higgins, loud enough now that people turned their heads from the minister. "You're the one. I seen you. I seen you on Penikese. I know you. You're a goddamned poxy leper. You brought it here and killed him with it and mean to kill the rest of us."

I backed away from Higgins, and the people around the grave backed away from me. He was shouting now. "You poxy bastard. You come here and killed him. Hell, you wasn't no better than to —"

Corbin Starkweather stepped toward him but Higgins caught up a spade and swung it hard. Corbin caught most of it on his back and arm and he went down. Then Higgins started for me, but the fresh-dug earth was slick mud now, and he went down, too, almost into the grave. I did the worst possible thing: I ran.

Around and over the tombstones and over the stonewall at the edge of the cemetery. My heart pounded faster than my feet, and then I heard the pounding behind me, but it came with John's voice, breathless, as he shouted, "I'm with you, Jack," and he was.

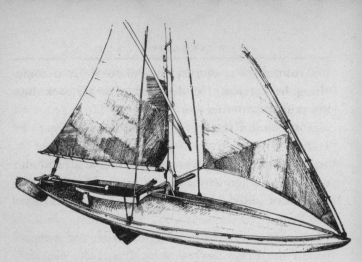

## CHAPTER SEVENTEEN

# The Weather Gage

THE CHICKEN HOUSE on Hiller Street gave up a startled clucking as we ran past it. Then we were at the head of our dock. The gangplank bent and boomed under the running, the dock float tipped and sloshed, and I was tearing at the dock lines for Skiff One.

Stop! I told myself. Think, do it right, and I closed my eyes for one breath and tried to think of Corbin Starkweather's hands working for him so quick but so neat. Okay.

John had gone through the house. The sound of

his running was clumsy, off-balanced from something he carried. He dropped a duffel sack into my skiff and another into Skiff Two. He gave me an almost comical shrug. "I guess it's time to go," he said.

"I just guess it is. I just guess." I have a bad habit of giggling when the sky is falling in. I pushed out and got the sails up. Number One had the gaff rig on her. I dropped the centerboard. The main went up first, pulling on the peak and throat halyards together until the throat was up. Then the peak halyard got cleated, leaving the gaff swinging horizontal until I swigged the throat good and tight with the gaff hoops rattling. Now the peak but not so tight. The mainsheet was free, the boom and gaff slatted back and forth as I snapped on the little jib. The rain sputtered on the canvas. My hands were working well and the little coils of line fell behind them like Corbin's. I pulled in the sheets and put the tiller over. The wind leaned into the sails and Skiff One spun around and shot away. Okay, I told myself, it's time to go.

John was behind me in Skiff Two and the wind was ahead of us as we went out. At Ram Island, though, he was abeam. Allen Plummer was right, the marconi rig and Herreshoff's new hardware were better to weather. I had one look back to Goosefish Cove before it was out of sight. It was time to go.

In formation, now, we beat. Out of the narrows in short tacks, one skiff turning a second after the other, thirty yards, shifting back again with a slap of canvas as the sails came around. Wind out of the northeast, the tack with the weather to port was longer. Once we turned the corner at Converse Point it would be a distant, bumpy reach to Penikese.

Skiff Two luffed and fell back beside me.

"You all right?" John shouted. I nodded and gave him thumbs up. He pointed to his sail. "He's right. Plummer's right." I nodded. He checked his sail and looked to me again, held up his duffel. "Stay warm." His shouts were small in the rain and wind, but reassuring. I nodded.

We came around off Planting Island Beach and it looked like we could fetch Converse Point. The foul-weather jacket from the duffel felt good and I needed it as we caught the change of seas that reaches in between the points when the Bay is up. You can feel it, even see it change from the regular rhythm of the harbor waves to the confused, lumpy chop that marks the edge of the real bay.

As we came up on Converse Point, a rider loped past the great, black and white mansion and out onto the lawn. The horse pulled up at the green skirt of grass and beach plum at the edge. The rider jumped down with her black skirt blowing. It was Ruth.

We passed close inshore. The trees shifted behind her as I sailed by, watching that face. I saw her suddenly stamp her foot. "Jack Stone, you get right back here!" I shook my head slowly, No. No. She did not stamp her foot this time. "Come back, Jack!" I raised one hand helplessly: I can't. There was a long moment when we just looked at each other, across the widening distance, then she raised one hand, Good-bye.

She was still there when the point grayed itself into the weather. We both watched till there was no point at all. Maybe that is why we didn't see One-armed Higgins until he was almost on us.

He must have run from the graveyard directly to his boat. It wasn't far, in Hiller's Cove south of Converse Point. He beat out to windward and waited. I had heard the Captain talk about it once, what every sailing warship tried to do to every other warship: seize the position to windward. It was called "taking the weather gage." We had Higgins to weather and the marsh at our backs. He could swoop down at us with the wind in his sails to block any escape. We had only one way out: upwind. I looked to John. He nodded and laid his arm toward the little boat. We came around and tightened up, beating for the shortest meeting with Higgins and hoping our slightly heavier, longer boats would go to weather better. If we could get past him we might lose him. Maybe. He saw us come around and he swooped.

His little gunning boat skimmed the waves, almost planing, and we thought we would make it past, but just before he reached us he spun the boat, leveled his shotgun and —

"Duck, Jack!"

I ducked, all right. The boom of his shotgun and a crack above my head came almost at once. I grabbed for the tiller and managed to keep Skiff One moving. A section of the starboard coaming was shattered just about where I had been. It wasn't bird shot, either, but big, pea-sized buckshot. Killing stuff. I peeked above the rail.

Higgins was beating, too, keeping ahead of us but barely. Jack was farther up toward him. Higgins rose on a wave, I looked back from my sail, he was turning quickly with the shotgun, I was ducking at the same time the second blast and boom hit. Sail, this time.

Higgins was good. Higgins was not stupid, either. He moved ahead of us using the waves as well as anyone could. He was getting ready for another pass. I could see him bailing with a can. He must be taking water. He should have taken care of one-eighteen. He turned and came again.

But John was faster. He had worked Skiff Two up

between Higgins and me. When Higgins turned, John turned. Higgins was coming down, trying to avoid him. John turned to run with Higgins and, just as the shotgun came up, he put the tiller over and rammed Higgins amidships. There was a loud wrenching of wood, the shotgun muzzles turned: two blasts. I bore off and tried to get some distance.

Higgins was too good. He was already away from John and coming at my boat. John scrambled to catch the shroud Higgins had blown apart. Skiff Two wallowed with her mast loose and was out of the battle until John could splice the shroud and tighten it again. Higgins set his rudder, bailed, reset it, bailed again. He was taking more water.

John had caught the shroud and was working a length of line to it. I was sailing as John had taught me, trying to get the best out of sail and boat and sea, but scared. Higgins was bailing and coming on, trying to get close enough to blow away Skiff One's transom, and me, with a double charge of buckshot.

Suddenly Corbin Starkweather's *Allise* came charging out of the rain with a leaping bow wave, heeling dangerously under every square foot of canvas it had, heavier and faster and more skillfully sailed than any of us, and it had the weather gage.

The shotgun was just coming up when Starkweather bellowed, "Higgins!"

Higgins looked back and his little boat faltered, catching a breaking wave over its deck. Higgins shook his head like a spaniel and screamed back, "Git, you fish scum! This is my doing! This leper dog killed my captain! I'm killing him!" He twisted in his seat and, resting the barrels on the stump of his left arm, fired both barrels aft.

The starboard handholds on *Allise*'s cabin house exploded and the torn canvas roof covering began to flutter. Starkweather came up from a crouch with his hand inside the rifle scabbard. "Fall off, Higgins!"

Higgins was reloading. I had tighened up into the wind and was moving away from the *Allise* and the gunning boat. John was moving again, toward me.

"Fall off, Higgins, or be paid!"

Higgins turned again, fired, and tore out a patch of sail where Starkweather's head had been. He waited with the other barrel. Corbin bobbed up and as quickly down, long enough to trigger the second shot. More sail gone.

Starkweather stood, tossing the rifle muzzle upward. The scabbard flew off and the wind caught it, turning it over and over like a lost blade of eelgrass in a current, slow and curving. His voice was distant now. "*Damn* it, Higgins! That *tears* it!"

John caught up to me, coming across and behind them and me. Go ahead, he waved frantically. Go! Get out of here! Move! I could not see the *Allise* or

Higgins behind his sail. I trimmed my sails and looked to my helming and we beat into the rain.

I heard the dull thud of a shotgun blast, then another. And then the single sharp crack of a rifle shot, and that was all I heard from the waters off Tinkham Marsh, that and the rain, the wind, the waves, and the roaring inside my own head.

There's not much after that.

John found Penikese in the rain. He was born to know that Bay. We worked along the shore until I found the beach. The tide was up.

I pointed to it and he nodded. I came about and sailed out, away from the beach. For some reason I did not want him to come in with me. Maybe I did not want him to see me so frightened. Maybe. He knew anyway.

We came around and were sailing in formation again. I waved him off, trying to be businesslike or something. He nodded. He started to raise his hand in the same sad way Ruth had, but he stopped because, after all, it wasn't good-bye.

I got the sails down and rowed in. I waited for a lull and beached her easy, then did a good job of furling up Allen Plummer's sail and lashing down the oars and spars. John would pick it up later, I figured. I could see Skiff Two reaching back and forth in the weather, waiting for Skiff One.

I shouldered the duffel and found the place. The

thought of what I was about to do frightens me more now than it did then. I must have been in some kind of shock to be so confident that I wouldn't get ground up in some closing pocket of time or space. I just sat down on the duffel and waited. Sat there like a dog under a porch.

There were no sheep this time, but it was the same lumpy, unpleasant ride. Skiff One was gone. The rain, the beach, the waves, the complaints of the gulls, looked like the same day I'd just left. But it wasn't the same.

I got back to Marion in just about the same way I got back before, except this time I rode on the flying bridge of a red power cruiser with a polyester sport from Onset who was glad to drop me off. It wasn't but twenty minutes out of his way and he was just out for a little ride, anyway. Fine as kind.

I found him out on the end of our dock, on that little roofed-over bench. It really wasn't so startling to see him old; I mean, I'd seen him before I left, hadn't I?

"Hello, John," I said.

He didn't turn for a few moments and I wondered if he'd gone deaf on me. But he hadn't. He finally looked around. "I've been waiting for you," he said. There were tears in his eyes.

"I just guess you have," I said. I guess there were tears in my eyes, too. We sat there and talked for the better part of an hour, until Doris wondered who was chatting on to old John Swain and came out and Almost Died.

## CHAPTER EIGHTEEN

# *Epilogue*

WELL, I LIED A LOT: about running away and signing on a freighter, and a lot of apologies, and Couldn't I Have Let Them Know, and not much at all from Will, which doesn't bother me as much as it did because he is mighty like Joshua and I can listen better to what he doesn't say. As for Doris, I was happy to see her. As to my sisters, they are, I am happy to report, still a pain in the neck.

What have I got to show for it all? Not much in the parts line: a set of oilskins that looks pretty good for being sewn up in 1902, a pair of button-fly over-alls, a canvas duffel, and a bone-handled knife engraved *Sam'l L. Clemens*. I've got a lot of other things that aren't so easy to show.

I've got my town, which I know in a new way. I know what it was and what it has become and I feel about it the way you'd feel about something you helped build. I figure that I still help to build it.

I've got the Bay, which I know in a new way. In some ways it doesn't change, though all the people around it have tried to change it. Or maybe they haven't tried hard enough not to change it. It is a part of some big natural magic, a force, a power, a sustainer. I know that I was born to know the Bay, too.

I know a lot of things in new ways. Sometimes I feel very old, sometimes I feel young. Mostly I feel impatient to get on with things because there's so much to do and so very little time. I know I've got this one life to work with, and it's mine. It's a one-shot, very personal affair and I'm going to do some interesting things with it.

Boats. I like boats and I like to work with my hands. I may be a good boat builder someday. John and I got the sheds cleaned out and the tools, all of the chestfuls of tools, polished and sharp again. We had started two skiffs and had begun getting brochures for a power planer and a good table saw when he died. I wish we could have had a big Rockwell planer when the Captain and Joshua and I were working together.

I buried him — we buried him, the family — on a rainy spring day in the cemetery near the Captain, 1904, and Joshua, 1933, and Minnie, 1942, and my grandmother, whose stone reads *Ruth Saltonstall Carter, Loving Wife, 1889–1952.*

I really hadn't known anything about my grandmother. It's strange how little you can bother to learn about your own family. She died before I was born, the stone says.

Once — it was on a late summer evening — I helped Ruth carry a basket of apples to her father's stable. We did not hurry on the way back and I held her hand. She laughed about something and I stopped and told her she was wonderful. She put her arm around me and her head on my shoulder and we walked almost all the way back to the house that way.

I love to think about that. I told John about it and he said, "She was, she was wonderful."

That's the best thing I have: John. To have a friend like John, even once in a life, is a lucky thing. He's dead now but, well, it's like the Bay. It changes and it doesn't change. It's part of some long, strong flow.

I've said enough. I think you'll find out for yourself. It's a mystery, the best kind, the kind that you must unravel for yourself, even if someone has already told you the butler did it. A mystery you don't ever solve, really.

And now I have this, written down, and I don't think I'll forget it or go crazy and not believe it. I'm putting it away for you, my grandson or my granddaughter, or both, or all, and when you are fifteen you can read it and wonder what old John Swain is going on about. Then you can find me on the end of the dock, on that little roofed-over bench, and we can talk it over.